Bananas
and Other Stories

by

Trixie Roberts

Published by Leaf by Leaf Press Ltd 2018

Copyright © Trixie Roberts 2018

ISBN 978-0-9957154-7-9

Acknowledgements

I am grateful to many people who have helped me during my writing life and in the production of this book. My thanks go to:

Barbara Ralphson, Dorothy Nelson and Mike Gregory who tutored me in my early writing days at Leigh and Bolton.

Elaine Dowling who typed many of the early drafts.

All members of the writing groups in both Ashton-in-Makerfield and Oswestry for their helpful criticisms and encouragement over the years.

My friend and neighbour Gill Hay for reading and helping with selection.

The members of Leaf by Leaf Press: Vicky Turrell, Ron Turner, John Heap, Wendy Lodwick Lowdon and Bernard Pearson for their forensic examination of my work and assistance in licking this book into shape.

Helen Baggott for proofreading.

My daughters: Gina for designing the book cover and oiling the wheels of publicity and Alice for putting the manuscript into a print-ready format.

Last and most, my husband Tony for enabling me to find time to write and providing meals, drinks and patient encouragement while I was doing so.

"Now I already have a hundred charms, thousands of magic formulas;
I found the charms in a hiding place, magic words from a cranny."

The Kalevala
17: 603-604

Dedication

To all storytellers, writers, listeners and readers who continue to value and champion the short story as a literary form.

Contents

Bananas 1

The Dummy Hand 15

Rosie O'Grady's 23

Daisy Hill 37

The Moss 45

Can You Get a Signal on York Minster? 55

The Brick Wall 65

Fish on Friday 71

Nude – circa 1920 77

Tuesday at Stella's 81

Late for Life 99

Guava with Garlic 103

Are We Nearly There Yet? 111

A Night at the Opera 121

Peace and War 131

Plan 141

Taking Off 151

Wisteria 161

Bananas

At our house, the one Jake and I bought when we were first married, the French doors give on to a terrace, facing south and west. In the early years of our life there, the rockeries and tubs were always full of summer colour and scents. I would sit there after garden work, breathing in the fragrance of honeysuckle and jasmine as they climbed the pergola. Our young daughters' summer play was surrounded by the reds and oranges of snapdragons and poppies. When they were babies I planted wild strawberries in the borders so that by the time they brought school friends, they were able to snack on the fruit whilst playing.

As the girls grew, so did the alfresco opportunities. Jake made a Wendy house at the end of the garden, beyond the fruit trees. This gave the girls endless fun and when they were older became a den in which they could gossip and sleep overnight with teenage friends. Meanwhile, I would never tire of spending all day outdoors planning and planting borders of marigolds, pinks and geraniums.

During dark, winter evenings by the fireside, I began to grieve for the foxgloves and hollyhocks of July. Winter soups simmering on the stove do not have the same appeal as the smell of the garden after a summer shower. My daughters started to buy me colourful plants for inside the house.

'This will give you something to grow without getting cold, Mum,' they said in unison one Christmas, presenting me with a large poinsettia and a jasmine the following Mother's Day. I soon had a growing collection of indoor bulbs, tropical flowering plants and ferns. At first, my interest in indoor gardening was limited. I had always had the odd busy Lizzie but without much enthusiasm. As these new arrivals were from my children, however, I tended them and watched them grow.

Jake was never a gardener. His twin passions are science fiction and listening to sport on the radio. He'd much rather have his nose in a novel than in the night-scented stock. But he seemed content to see me moving around the house with misting spray and Baby-Bio.

'Just ignore me and work around me,' he would say whilst listening to the Test Match. Although he had probably encouraged the children to give me the house plants initially, it was not an interest we ever shared. But then, I could never understand the appeal of listening to spectator sports on the radio.

Miss Robb arrived in town as our new librarian. She was a breath of fresh air, following decades of the retiring and now retired Mr Sleight. As she became aware of Jake's and my interests, she began to extend the ranges of books on science fiction and gardening. As a keen gardener herself, Miss Robb was always able to suggest the right books for every topic, from passion flowers to pH levels. My plants thrived and grew in number and size. It was difficult to manage house plants as well as the garden. I had little time for anything else and my daughters became very good cooks out of necessity.

'Maybe you could grow some fruit and veg then

there will always be something to eat and we won't have to disturb you?' they said.

I had, by now, taken to indoor gardening like a Venus fly-trap to a passing insect. It kept me happy and busy all year round. No waiting for the frosts to pass or the winds to die down. This gave me the opportunity to think of the floor plan of the house as a garden. I built a rockery in one corner of the conservatory and the long, draughty rear porch was transformed by a border of early spring bulbs.

Despite my attempts to plan a good aquatic ecosystem from the beginning, we became troubled by an increase in the number of insects around the indoor pond. I was advised that the introduction of more predators, such as tadpoles, would provide its own solution. But when the baby frogs decided it was time to leave the pool en masse I rather wished I had stuck with the insects. The frogs hid everywhere.

'My pyjamas were jumping around the bedroom this morning,' laughed Jake. I left the French doors open for days on end, hoping the frogs would find an escape route to the great outdoors. Instead they found their way to the kitchen and hid under cabbage and leeks in the vegetable rack, only to be disturbed and start hopping around the kitchen as soon as a meal was being prepared. They were so well camouflaged against our indoor turf, I took to sprinkling salt in front of me whenever I walked on it so as to make them jump out of the way and make a path.

We had long ago given up plans to decorate any of the walls as they were covered in climbers. When we invited friends to supper, sometimes there wasn't enough space to sit and eat as all the tables were covered with seed trays and pots of cuttings. The problem solved itself after a time, as fewer and fewer and then no more of our invitations were accepted. Such a pity, just as the girls were perfecting new dishes. Their frog's legs were particularly delicious.

Then some of the growing was done. The girls left home. One to university and the other to work abroad as an au pair. Before they left they gave Jake a personal stereo with headphones, so he could listen to sport on the radio wherever he liked. They gave me a young banana tree in an enormous pot. I had to think carefully where to put it. A banana needs light and height but the growth of my ferns had begun to cover the windows, preventing light from reaching some of the plants I already had. The young tree's arrival forced me to address the problem so I had more windows cut into the walls at all levels. Now the sides of the house were fully glazed and the whole place looked like a palm-house. As upstairs was still relatively clear of window-hugging plants, there was enough light for growing bananas.

My indoor work meant I had neglected the outdoor trees and shrubs and they became overgrown, like a massive hedgerow as if in competition with the plants indoors. Subsequently there was an increase in wildlife including birds of prey. A tawny owl took to visiting and hunting right by the rear porch. He would sit and stare at me through the window. If I spoke to him he would put his head on one side and give me a quizzical look. I took to leaving the back door open and he would sometimes fly around inside for a while: with all those frogs it was a good hunting ground.

One day I answered a knock at the door to find Mrs Lester from a few doors away. She explained that a few of the neighbours were concerned as they hadn't seen Jake or me for some days. I laughed and said I hadn't seen much of Jake either. He was fully occupied listening to the Winter Olympics broadcasts and I had simply been too busy germinating geraniums. Perhaps she would like one? She accepted my invitation to come in but didn't stay long. She seemed bemused when she looked around inside the house and left very quickly after a lizard crawled from the poolside, and slithered over her feet. I reassured her it wasn't poisonous but she made off in a great hurry mumbling something about a fruitcake.

The following summer Jake and I had to barbecue our meals in the garden, as the kitchen oven was the only place suitable for raising a particularly tender tropical orchid. Sometimes there were no meals at all, as I wasn't aware of his return home from work. He was now reading so much science fiction that he was visiting the library almost every evening. It seemed Miss Robb always had something new for him. At home it was becoming difficult to find each other. Sometimes I would spot him, through the foliage, lost in the latest publication or listening to… er… golf on the radio.

Our life had become very quiet. Not only had our teenagers gone, but their friends too. No shrieking and laughter from the den in the school holidays. No more endless interruptions to the day, with requests for money, clean jeans or yet more ingredients for a meal.

'Is there anything we can cook tonight?' had been a regular cry.

I did have more time to concentrate on growing new species. I even experimented in crossing various strains to develop new types of plant and wrote up my findings. This generated some interest among other gardeners and I became quite well known in amateur circles. Miss Robb was happy to be a self-

8

styled agent: a clearing-house for enquiries from other green-fingered library users. Her help was useful and enabled me to concentrate on my plants and writing. She kept me very busy but Jake was happy to walk down to the library at any time to act as messenger.

A journalist asked if he could visit and interview me for a magazine article. Although I agreed, the meeting never took place as, when he and his photographer arrived, I was unable to open the door owing to the tangle of overnight growth in the porch. As I struggled with the shears I saw the crew walking away, no doubt in the belief that they were at the wrong house. Then they started to run. I think they were surprised by the family of bats now occupying the eaves behind the wisteria. The owl visits less often now as the tangled growth restricts his flying but he still stares at me from the branches outside. He's now acquired a family. I was pruning the indoor rambler rose in order to get to the kitchen and saw them: a whole row of owls, staring at me.

I have never been able to share Jake's passion for

science fiction as it seems so disposable. The books are here today, gone back to the library tomorrow. Plants are not a bit like this: they never repeat themselves. In the same way that young children grow, learn and respond, an individual plant is never the same two days running. There will always be some change in the way the leaves hang and the flowers hold themselves. Turn a specimen in from the light and it will shift position again, taking on a different stance as if altered by the experience. Buds bloom and young branches shoot with more new leaves and buds. Until the growing starts, one never knows how things will develop.

The banana tree grew taller. Originally, I had put it in the dining room, believing that when it eventually fruited, we could pick as we wished to eat, but soon it had to move to the hall, so it could grow up into the stairwell and get light from the upper windows. Eventually, this was not enough so I cut a hole in the ceiling to accommodate it.

The next winter, Jake caught a bad dose of flu and had to have a few days off work. As he was confined to bed, I had no difficulty in finding him. Thinking I would cheer him up, I chopped my way out and went to the library for some books. It was Miss Robb's day off so I just chose six at random. He had read them all before. The next day I went back, this time with a begonia cutting for Miss Robb and asked her advice about Jake's recent borrowing habits. She amazed me by knowing everything he had and hadn't read, going all the way back to Jules Verne. She certainly knows what he enjoys. Jake was delighted to have the new books so I felt comfortable leaving him to recuperate and read while I cultivated cacti. Before his return to work, there was a mild spell of weather and Jake felt well enough to sit outside in the fresh air. He decided to spruce up the now redundant den and read in the shelter when it became chilly. This seemed an excellent idea but he surprised me by flatly refusing to let me put any plants in it. I had never known him be so positive in his refusal of anything before, even when I pointed out how bare the inside looked now that the girls' posters had gone.

'No. You have enough to do with the plants in the house without having to come in here as well.' He wouldn't even agree to a window box.

The banana tree's top branches began to fill the attic so I had a glass dome built on the roof. Now the tree is spreading beautifully at the top and I jump on to it from the landing and climb it to reach the fruit. An extremely vigorous creeper puts out new growth which blocks the landing overnight. I have taken to sleeping with a pair of shears by the bed so I can be sure of getting out in the morning. Like Sleeping Beauty's prince fighting his way through the briars, I cut myself a route to the bathroom. Jake sleeps most nights in the den, preferring not to disturb me as he listens to the sailing on the radio, whilst lost in Miss Robb's recommendations. Sometimes I feel the need to look at the outside world so I climb the banana tree and gaze through the dome at the night sky. It's very soothing up there, enjoying a banana and contemplating the moon.

I miss the letters from my girls. I'm sure they still

write but the postman can no longer get near the house to deliver anything. On some nights my memories of them are overwhelming as I imagine I can hear giggling coming from the den. As I sleep alone, I am glad of the growth which has grown around the outside of the house. There is a hedge of thorny bramble and I feel safe inside. It's also good insulation for my tropical specimens. It's grown so thick it's now almost impossible for Jake to pass to and fro at all. If he does come in I can't see him for plants and he can't hear me for his radio. I haven't seen him for weeks now but I'm sure he's snug in his den, absorbed in Miss Robb's latest suggestions, peacefully listening to the, er... competitive angling.

The Dummy Hand

There was no light in the house. Three black storeys and a cellar. There had been no sign of life for days but, in any case, Carl could sniff out a promising house by instinct, just as it was second nature to him to slip a latch and be able to find his way round inside, silently and in darkness. This house looked safe enough. He needed an easy one to get him started again: his first job since Strangeways.

He had already walked past the house at different times of day and in various disguises. He had waited at the bus stop over the road, pretended to be a taxi driver waiting for a fare and spent quite a while in workman's clothes checking the hydrant just outside the front gate. The house was at the end of a Georgian terrace so by walking round the side and back, Carl had assessed entry points and worked out an approximate floor plan based on the pattern of windows, doors and chimneys.

Although he felt rusty, Carl went through the

breaking and entering procedure swiftly: it was as automatic as shaving or brushing his teeth. First he went into a room with a window at the side of the house. This overlooked a narrow strip of garden bordered by a high wall so he could safely turn on his torch without being visible from outside. It was a fairly small room with a sewing machine, a chest with multiple drawers and a bookcase full of sewing patterns. Carl moved against the walls into the hall. Years ago he had been told by Charlie, a fellow prisoner, to move along walls with his back to them and he always did. Charlie had said,

'If you can hear someone say, "I'm right behind you," you're in trouble. Never let anyone get behind you.' Carl had remembered it ever since.

The hall was large enough to accommodate bookshelves which were lit by the street lamp shining in through the fanlight above the door. There were some fairly mundane reference books but also some beautiful antique volumes. Books were not Carl's speciality; he was a silver man but the fact that the valuable books were there convinced him that his instinct had been right; there were things to be found in this house.

He slipped into a room on the other side of the hall. This was a large sitting room, richly decorated and furnished. At one end was a desk with a computer and a shelf with more books but these were manuals by business gurus like Bill Gates. Towards the front of the room was a rosewood table with several decanters of spirits. Sampling the drink in a house was always Carl's little indulgence. He would argue that the quality of the whisky indicated the value of the goods. He found a crystal glass in a bow-fronted cabinet, poured himself a generous measure and allowed himself to sink into one of the most comfortable armchairs he had ever sat in. He let the whisky warm him down to his feet while his eyes became accustomed to the room's features with only the light from the street lamp. On the coffee table in front of him were the things that made this job worthwhile. A silver ashtray, a set of coasters and a fruit bowl, probably Edwardian: very nice pieces. The box containing playing cards was Georgian by the look of it and the snuffbox certainly was; beautifully worked and heavy. Carl knew these items were things his old contacts would be interested in buying. This would be enough for one night; he wouldn't even venture upstairs, no risks, he'd just enjoy his whisky and be off.

He was studying the design on the card box when he noticed two more whisky glasses on the table and, they weren't empty.

'So,' Carl thought, 'I've got company.' He soon spotted one pair of feet poking out from the bottom of the curtains and started looking round for the other. His chair was backed against the wall so there was no danger anyone could be behind him. Then he noticed a swivel chair, facing the opposite wall, away from him. The feet were under that. Right by the chair was a standard lamp with a fringe of tassels hanging down from the shade. The tassels were moving rhythmically in response to the slightest of breaths coming and going underneath it. Carl was thinking quickly; there were two of them; what if they were armed? He never used firearms, that wasn't his game, but he'd met plenty of young hotheads in prison who would take guns out with them. Carl was proud of being an old fashioned professional; he used his hands to examine and remove ashtrays, cream jugs and candlesticks, not to threaten with guns. Then the tassels jumped and danced to the accompaniment of an enormous sneeze, and then another. Carl shot to his feet and moved towards the door. The swivel chair turned and a torch was flashed in Carl's face.

'Blimey, if it isn't Cat-burglar Carl. Just look here, Eric.' The feet came out from behind the curtain.

'Well, well, well. We thought you were still inside. When did you get out?'

Carl faced two men he hadn't seen since Strangeways. Tom and Eric Gray, twins who always worked together, and therefore, always did time together. They had been released some time before Carl.

'Tom, Eric, what a surprise,' said Carl. 'Only been out a few weeks. I've been lying low and looking for a safe job. Thought I'd take it easy for a while, don't fancy doing time again. How about you?'

'Same really. This looked likely; no one here at the moment. Quiet neighbourhood; no one on that side.'

'Have you diamond men found anything?'

'No we've not been upstairs yet, we got waylaid by this scotch. It's jolly good. There's some nice silver here for you, Carl. You take that, we'll find our jewels and we'll split anything else we can carry. OK?'

'Done.'

'There's no rush,' said Tom. 'I think we should have another drink to celebrate old times.'

'Let's see if there are any cards in this box,' said Carl. 'We could have a hand or two, just like the old days in Strangeways.'

'Pity old Charlie's not here to make up the numbers,' said Eric.

'You mean "I'm right behind you" Charlie? He always used to win,' said Tom. 'We're better off with a dummy hand. Here, Carl, pass your glass, I'll be barman. You dealin', Eric?'

'Anyone heard anything about Charlie lately?'

'He got out ages before me,' said Carl. 'But you know Charlie, always said he wasn't hanging around. He planned to hop off to Spain. He had a stash somewhere I reckon.'

'Probably won it playing cards,' laughed Eric. 'He was sharp was Charlie. If we'd been playing for money in there, he'd have cleaned us out.'

The three men were able to see the cards well enough and soon dropped into their familiar ways of playing together and exchanging banter as if they were still in a Strangeways cell. So comfortable were they that they had completely lost sight of the purpose for which they had come. Tom had to keep nudging Eric as he nodded off.

'Come on, Eric. We'll have two dummy hands if you fall asleep.'

Carl wasn't at all worried that he hadn't yet made a profit out of the night. He was content that he had successfully managed to get into the house and stayed undetected for so long. He hadn't lost his touch after all. Meeting Tom and Eric again was a bonus. The friends didn't notice that they were halfway down the second decanter of whisky. They didn't notice the dawn light creeping in at the windows. They didn't even notice the tassels on the lampshade dance as the taxi doors slammed outside or the keys tinkling as the front door was opened. They were alerted only when they heard voices in the hall.

'I'm going straight up, love. Let's just leave the cases here, I'll sort them out in the morning.'

'OK, sweetheart, I'm just going to check the emails then I'll be right behind you.'

The footsteps were outside the door and all Carl, Tom and Eric could do was stare at the newcomer as he turned on the light.

'Well, well, well, lads,' said Charlie. 'You'd better deal me in.'

Rosie O'Grady's

Soul, passion and coconut-shy drama could always be found at Rosie O'Grady's; the bar with the worst beer in town and the most decibels, especially late on a Saturday after a bad day at the races. Market traders in from the country trying to make a living and smart, young men trying to make an impression, shared the brass bar rail with locals. Anyone harbouring a simmering vendetta seemed to wait until they reached Rosie's before settling matters. Battles were fought to the accompaniment of Eliza on the honky-tonk piano. Waitresses dodged flying matchwood chairs and backgammon boards to serve evil looking dishes of 'Rick's rabbit stew'. Rick, Rosie's chef, had learned his kitchen-craft while serving time for grievous bodily harm. No one dared question the provenance of the rabbit.

The whole bar was always in motion, waitresses, customers and dancers swaying past each other like young otters learning to work the river. Not even the air rested; smoke coils went upwards and hovered over the activity. The more innocent of the young patrons must have wondered if the rocking of the ceiling gas lamps was because of the rag-time or the rumbles. They soon discovered the reason when after an initial looking over by Rosie to make sure there were no guns in their pockets, she allowed her girls to introduce them to the red-curtained activities upstairs. The girls selected their clients with care, tempting only those whose wallets were full after a good day at the races.

There was a stage in the bar where various entertainments were held, country music, karaoke nights, and the most popular of all on a Friday, was burlesque night. Some of Rosie's girls who worked upstairs during the week had spent time (or as they would say, 'done time') working in burlesque clubs in the city and adapted what they had learned to the tastes of Rosie's customers.

There was to be a big race meeting the following Friday and Rosie knew they would be busy. She wanted a special stage act to encourage the lucky punters with money, to spend it in her bar. She phoned Brett, her theatrical agent.

'Just one night, Friday. My girls are brilliant but they'll be busy upstairs too so I need reserves. Yes, and one burlesque act with a difference. I need something a bit special.'

'No worries, Rosie, I have the very thing. Scheherazade. She's the best burlesque act this side of the Mississippi. You'll love her. Do you have a secure dressing room?' This was something Rosie hadn't expected. Usually, the performers used an old caravan behind the kitchens to change and make-up.

'Oh sure, Brett. Don't worry about that. She'll be safe with us.'

'Scheherazade can take care of herself. It's what she uses in her act that needs to be kept under lock and key.'

Rosie was suitably reassuring and Scheherazade was booked.

Rosie had a word with Tommy, the barman, then went to the kitchens.

'Now, Rick. We'll be busy on Friday night. All

hungry after the races and wanting to hang around cos of the burlesque so perhaps you could rustle up some tempting dishes for the menu as alternatives to rabbit? I'll leave it to you. See what you can get at the market then just ask Tommy to write it on the blackboard before they all start arriving.' Rick had learned many skills in prison but literacy wasn't one of them.

'Sure, Rosie, I'll give 'em something tasty.'

'Oh, and Rick. Do you want to ask your mate to come and help you out in the kitchen? Double time after 10 o'clock and a free supper.'

'He'll be there,' reassured Rick. 'He never turns down free food and a bit of extra cash.' This mate, real name Rod, had also served time with Rick. He was a cat burglar turned kitchen hand. The two men's skills, however, were different. Rick was the creative chef whereas Rod turned out to be an excellent butcher. He could chop, slice and cut meat, fish and vegetables with great speed. This reputation earned him the name of 'Lightnin' Rod' and he was often drafted in to help at local diners and function rooms during busy times. His prep work was good and quick so he didn't need paying for too many hours. Rosie was on a safe bet offering double time after 10. It was unlikely Rod would be around beyond 8.30.

After Rosie returned to update the girls about Friday, Rick stopped and shared a smoke with Tommy.

'Have you heard about the guest performer on Friday?' Tommy asked Rick. 'She's called Scheherazade. They say her act is unique.'

Rick looked surprised then laughed. 'Scheherazade? She still at it? I know her from way back; her act's really wild. If Rosie puts her name on the posters round the racecourse, we'll get a full house alright.'

On Friday afternoon, a cab drew up and Scheherazade got out. She had with her, her costume box and an enormous case on wheels. Rosie took her to the caravan. Scheherazade seemed disappointed with the accommodation, especially when she learnt she was going to have to share it with all the other girls.

'Still, as long as Romeo is safe.'

'Romeo?' Rosie questioned.

'Sure, he's an important part of my act. Come and see.' She opened the case which contained a cage. Inside it was coiled an enormous python. 'There,' Scheherazade pointed to Romeo. 'Isn't he magnificent? He's got a massive girth and such a beautiful pattern on his skin.'

Rosie could see this was true but was uneasy when the python stared straight at her. 'You take him on stage? How do you know he won't escape into the audience? I don't want my customers upset... or worse.'

'No problem,' reassured Scheherazade. 'He's very tame and well trained. I've had him for years. To be honest he's getting a bit old and slower now but that makes him easier to work with. As soon as the act is over, he goes straight back in the cage which is locked. I always have the key on me, even in my stage costume.'

'Well, I'll have to take your word for it. Make sure the cage is locked now and I'll take you to meet the other girls in the show.'

Rosie left Scheherazade comparing notes with the girls about their experiences in the city. In the bar, she saw the newly chalked up menu with, as she had hoped, a few alternatives to rabbit stew. One item caught her eye so she went to look for Rick.

'Rick, I like the look of tonight's menu but isn't swordfish and horseradish sauce a rather odd combination?'

'Sure it's original but it's easy and cheap,' he said, pointing over to the field beyond the boundary fence. 'Horseradish is growing wild there and it will add some bite.'

Rosie knew Rick could work miracles in the kitchen so, whilst she was not entirely convinced, she let it pass.

Evening approached and the crowds started to come up from the racecourse.

'Lots of smiling faces,' thought Rosie. 'A good sign.'

Tommy at the bar was already engaged with the first customers.

'Yeah, I did well today.' A man in a smart jacket volunteered this information as he ordered a double whisky. 'So did plenty of others. A few favourites fell or did badly so outsiders came through. There are some sad bookies tonight but lots of happy gamblers.'

'That's what we like to hear,' smiled Tommy handing over the drink and pocketing the change he had been told to keep.

Rick and the kitchen staff were busy preparing for lots of diners, hungry after a day in the fresh air yelling at horses and jockeys. As yet, the girls upstairs weren't very busy as most of the punters were waiting for the floor show later. Scheherazade was top of the bill. In her office, Rosie was counting the first batch of the evening's takings to put in the safe when she heard a low-throated scream of horror. Her first thought was that Rick had lost his rag in the kitchen and threatened someone. Maybe a night like this was too much responsibility? She ran to the kitchen but all she could see was steamy activity accompanied by a lot of good natured banter.

'Did you hear that scream?'

'Sounded like it came from over there,' said Rick pointing towards the caravan. 'Perhaps Miss Scheherazade's unwell?' Then they heard wailing and sobbing. Rick returned to the demands of the kitchen and Rosie ran to the caravan.

Scheherazade was in her dressing gown, standing distraught beside the empty cage.

'Romeo's gone. How could he have escaped? The cage was locked.'

'Jumpin' prairie dogs.' Rosie went white. 'He could be anywhere.'

'Well he's very visible,' snapped Scheherazade. 'If he's gone into your bar he would be noticed.'

'That's what worries me,' said Rosie, thinking quickly. 'Hey, does he like horseradish? He may have made for the field over there; it's full of it.'

Scheherazade started to wail.

'We'll never find him in there. It's getting dark.'

'Look,' Rosie was thinking quickly, 'I'll go and start a discreet search for him. You get ready for the stage and work on an act without Romeo.'

'That's the problem. I'm not as young as I was. It's difficult to do the more athletic movements now. Romeo adds a touch of spice to the act without my having to do too much.'

'Well, you'll have to think of something. I've got a bar full of men with bulging wallets waiting to have their fancy tickled.'

'How's Scheherazade going to do her act?' the kitchen hand asked as Rosie pulled her from the kitchen to help in the search for the python.

'That's her problem. What we've got to do is make sure we see Romeo before any of the punters do.' They found torches and headed for the yard.

'Who is it?' Scheherazade, still upset but getting dressed for the stage, replied to the knock at the door.

'I'm from the kitchen. I've brought you a drink and perhaps I can help.'

'I doubt it but thank you anyway. Come in.'

Rick stood in the doorway. 'Surprise, surprise. Hi, baby.'

'Rick, Rick. It can't be! Is it really you? I didn't

32

know you were out.'

She ran to him and they kissed enthusiastically.

'Been out a while but didn't know where you were. Rosie gave me a chance working here so I decided to knuckle down, save some money and then... start to look for you. So you're still travelling with the act.'

'I've had to earn a living, Rick. But I'm not sure how I'm going to do that now if Romeo isn't found.'

'Rosie's doing a search here now and we'll have a look around the field in the morning. I'll take some bait.'

'But I can't do my act tonight.' Scheherazade was tearful.

'I can help there. Just step outside with me.'

Rick led her to his caravan on the far side of the yard. In the corner of the living area was a large cage and inside were two magnificent parrots.

'Oh, Rick, you still have Blue Lagoon and Pink Gin.'

'Yes, Mamma did a good job of looking after them while I was inside. You could use them tonight if you like.'

'But it's years since they were on stage.'

'They're bright birds. They won't have forgotten what to do. Here, try.'

Rick put a record on his old gramophone and the birds immediately looked animated. He opened the cage and Scheherazade reached in. The parrots came to her straight away. She began to move to the music and the parrots knew exactly what to do. Where they should perch when Scheherazade needed her hands to undo a button or loosen a lace; where to fan out their wings strategically. 'They'll save the day,' reassured Rick. 'And after the show, you can relax here with me and a nightcap.'

When Scheherazade's act began, Rosie was visibly relieved. There was no sign of Romeo but Blue Lagoon and Pink Gin were a great success with the audience. Greg Major, an old friend of Rosie's and local garage owner, had just bought her a drink at the bar.

'Come on, Rosie. You've been on your feet all night. Sit here with me a few minutes while I watch this clever girl.'

'Thanks, Greg. I think I shall. It's been a murderous day. Have you had your supper?'

'Yes. Really unusual. I've never had swordfish before. I didn't know it had such an interesting pattern on the skin.'

'Really? No, me neither.'

When Scheherazade's act was over, Rosie took a bottle of whisky from the bar and turned to Greg.

'Come into my office, Greg, and give me a hand with this.' Greg looked at the bottle and then at the cash box Rosie had just taken from Tommy. 'It's time to count up the next lot of takings.'

Sometime after the show finished and the kitchen closed, Eliza was still playing her full repertoire of piano rags. The bar was doing good trade as were the girls upstairs. Rick and Scheherazade were making love in Rick's caravan watched over by the parrots. Rosie and Greg, having counted another tidy sum were reminiscing and enjoying the whisky. Despite the relaxed feeling it gave her and the pleasure of a few, rare moments of relaxation with an old friend,

Rosie still had a few questions buzzing round in her head.

Scheherazade kept Romeo's cage locked and carried the key at all times. How could he have escaped? How did Scheherazade get hold of Rick's parrots and train them in time for the show? He was so protective of them. And she had certainly underestimated Rick's enterprise in obtaining a supply of swordfish, when Rosie O'Grady's was over three hundred miles from the ocean.

Daisy Hill

Elizabeth walks along the main road. There's a lot of traffic this afternoon but the lollipop lady's by the crossing. She goes up to her.

'Hello. It's busy today.'

'It will be even busier when they let the kids loose. Do you want to cross, love? Here, I'll see you over. Nice day. Funny how it always turns nice when the holidays are over and they have to go back to school.'

Elizabeth just says, 'Thank you.'

She makes her way to the baker's shop on the corner of the lane leading to Daisy Hill. She wonders if there will be any whinberry tarts left. If not, perhaps she'll get an Eccles cake. Whinberry tarts are her favourite; they are sweet and the juice stains your teeth and fingers. Mam would get cross if you spilt any on your clean dress. She stands outside the shop. Its sign reads, 'Tina's Tanning Parlour'. There are no cakes in the window. A young woman is inside sitting on a high stool. She is filing her nails and staring at Elizabeth. That's funny. We used to do the tanning in the barn at the back of Sutton's farm. It was never called a parlour. The parlour was where you put the visitors. Where's the baker's gone?

She looks around and the sign saying Daisy Hill reminds her where she's going. She starts to walk away from the main road and up the hill. There are no daisies. All these houses never used to be here. It was all open land and footpaths before you got up to the woods and then the farms beyond. Elizabeth remembers picking whinberries and then blackberries when they came ripe in September. They made lovely pies, with apple. We used to collect them in cans to take home on baking day. She looks up the hill. The road between the houses follows the same way that the old path did and she sees there are still trees up the hill beyond. She carries on walking.

A young woman comes out of one of the houses and struggles to settle a toddler in a pushchair.

'Sit down, Jamie. We have to get to school to

collect Megan.' The woman doesn't recognise Elizabeth as one of her neighbours. Despite the fact that she's in a hurry, she hesitates when she notices Elizabeth is wearing slippers.

'You OK, dear?'

'Oh yes, thank you. I've just got to get back home. Mam will be wondering where I've got to. Nice day.'

'Take care,' says the young woman, clearly uneasy but having to rush on.

There's a house with a large lawn and garden furniture. Elizabeth notices tea things on the table. Tea time. She goes up to the table and starts to drink a mug of tea. A woman comes out of the house with a magazine. She stares at Elizabeth.

'Hello. Can I help you?'

'Hello. Nice day. Is it tea time? I should be getting home to Mam's.'

'Why don't you sit down and rest a minute? I'll just go in and get you a fresh cup.' She runs back into the house. This tea's not very nice; no sugar. Elizabeth doesn't want a fresh cup so she leaves and carries on walking up the hill.

Elizabeth reaches the woods. There's a bench on the walkway skirting the woods, a little way from the main path. She sits down. The bench overlooks the new houses and Elizabeth can see the way she's just walked all the way back down to the main road. There are lines of children crossing with the lollipop lady. The sun feels warm on her face. She shuts her eyes and remembers: this is where we used to climb trees and collect conkers. On top of the world; Daisy Hill was our Empire. Can't climb the trees now. All those daisy chains; we made hundreds of them while the boys had conker fights. Then we'd pick whinberries and blackberries. Lovely long summers we had. I wonder if Mam's made any pies today? A bee buzzes by and Elizabeth sits up with a start.

She looks down to the houses and sees a police car in the street. One policeman is talking to the woman with the pushchair who now has another child with her. Another policeman is in the garden of the woman who has tea with no sugar. Elizabeth sees an ambulance. She cries out.

'Oh no. An ambulance. It's Jack. Is he going to be

alright? Have they told Mam?' She gets up and starts to run further up Daisy Hill. 'I'm coming. I'm coming.' She can't run well and one of her slippers comes off and she falls over. It's hard to get up. She can't. 'How am I going to get home now? I'm stuck.'

Three boys come along on bikes, laughing like boys on bikes do.

'Is that you, Jack? Are you alright? I've got to get up to Mam's.'

The boys get off their bikes and come towards her. They start to help her up but then one says, 'It may not be a good idea to move her in case something's broken. We learnt it in Scouts. Don't worry, Missus. We'll get help. I'll go to the police back there. You two stay with her.'

Elizabeth still struggles to get up.

'But I've got to get to Mam's. Where's Jack? Is he alright?'

One of the boys retrieves her lost slipper. Then they sit beside her on the ground and succeed in getting her to lie still.

'Help's on its way, Missus. You'll be OK,' they say.

A policeman joins the paramedics who climb the hill with a stretcher and they carry her down to the ambulance.

'We'll get her checked over but it doesn't look like anything's broken. Ring The Willows and let them know we've found her, thanks to half the population of Daisy Hill. We'll soon have you home, love.'

Later that evening, Susie, the care worker, is helping Elizabeth get ready for bed after a hot bath.

'Not much of a bruise, Elizabeth. It might ache for a few days, that's all. What a scare you gave us this afternoon, taking off up Daisy Hill.'

Elizabeth stares.

'Daisy Hill. Did I get to Mam's?'

'I don't know but you came home in an ambulance.'

'Did I?'

'Yes. Followed by a police car.'

'Did I?'

'Lovely young policeman came in with you to talk to Matron. You know how to pick 'em, Elizabeth.'

'Do I?'

'Come on. Let's get you into bed and I'll bring you some cocoa.'

The Moss

The train journey took twenty minutes from Marshend to town. Richard enjoyed the twice daily trip; a buffer zone between porridge-faced children and city office: a brief escape from them both. Here was a chance to flick through the paper, attempt the crossword, or read the report on the Rovers match the previous night. Sometimes he simply stared out of the window and gazed at the landscape, soothed into daydreams or even to sleep by the carriage's motion of lullaby-lilt.

For much of the twenty minutes the train crossed the moss, a wetland where trees and shrubs were occasional and struggling. After heavy rain, the ponds ran into each other so Richard imagined they were travelling on a hydrofoil. Sometimes the sunlight made the brown scrubby land look scorched. Here and there a marked-out plot was a memorial to the attempts of a persistent farmer, or maybe a succession of optimistic ones to defy nature and grow potatoes or turnips. Most mornings, mist hovered just above the ground. Richard could see a receding succession of features; marsh, scrub, the motorway and beyond, the mill chimneys and office blocks of Hebbleton, each layer of the panorama air-brushed to the next with mist. It had been a great feat of engineering to lay track across this land almost two hundred years ago. The few buildings visible from the track were the long abandoned cottages of the peat cutters. These houses formed derelict clusters around the old stopping places where today's Sprinter trains no longer stopped. There was one pub, The Leaking Boot, but who drank in it now was a mystery. Richard could never remember seeing it open.

Over the time he had been commuting, the journey's features had been mapped on to Richard's memory. The sequence of marsh and moss, scrub and signal box was so well known to him that if he came round from dozing he would know exactly which point they had reached before opening his eyes.

In the carriage the passengers shared a familiarity because of their common daily encounter. There were plenty of men in suits, boys in the uniform of the cathedral school where Richard hoped his sons would go when older. A young woman with spiked hair and a pierced nose often sat at the back chatting and giggling with the young guard who was always cheerful and would almost dance through the carriages checking the tickets. There was a woman who rode with a girl in a wheelchair, only on Thursdays; sometimes Richard helped her. During the journey, nobody spoke, no names were known but all knew where each sat on the passage between home and work. Annual holidays meant there were gaps; more room for Richard to spread out and doze.

Richard often tried to imagine what the mosses had been like before the railway. How life was lived by the peat cutters and farmers before 20th century consequences of the 19th century railway had carved them away. He had seen an exhibition at the museum about their way of life. There were maps, artefacts and some old photographs. Two men outside a cottage with their horse and cart. They were wearing rough cloth coats and knitted gloves. Thick socks came over their boots. There was a picture of the inside of a cottage with a woman and a child standing by a fireplace. A peat fire, not blazing but apparently steaming. Everything was damp and dark. Monochrome sepia. Richard would have hated to bring up a family in that humid, unhealthy atmosphere. What he provided for his own family was not grand but they were warm and dry and his wife cooked wholesome meals. These cutters had led their lives alongside a high water table and even that had been drowned under the changes brought by the railway. They had been displaced only to be rehoused much later in a museum.

With the onset of winter, both daily journeys took place in the dark. Richard began to daydream about the family Christmas at home. Hardly anything could be seen out of the train windows. The mosses were black, no street lights, no inhabited houses, only pools reflecting the moon.

One morning Richard became aware of an unfamiliar passenger, a small, round man with a beard. His clothes were rough and shabby; Richard thought he must be a tramp. Once the train had left Marshend and was out in the open country, the man started to pace up and down the carriage, looking out and scanning the dim landscape. Richard was aware of the smell of damp wool and potatoes. As they passed some old cottages by a signal box the man sat down and stared out into the mosses around it. He was there the next day and the next and behaved in exactly the same way. Everyone got used to him; he became a regular. Then a day of driving rain slowed the train down to a crawl at certain points along the way. Richard came round from a daydream and realised the strange man was no longer on the train. A few days later, Richard was dozing again, lethargic after celebrating Rovers' 4-0 victory the night before. Heavy rain was running down the windows so the landscape was a soggy blur. Through the water Richard thought he saw the man standing in the doorway of The Leaking Boot.

Then he fell back into his reverie of the heavenly fourth goal and how it wouldn't be long before his boys would be old enough to go to the match with him. He had a fantasy that he was part of the Rovers team, playing a charity match against an amateur eleven from The Leaking Boot.

Spring arrived and the journeys were wet as snows melted and merged with the marshes. The train water-skied along. Sometimes, Richard thought he caught a glimpse of the strange man out on the mosses, but when he blinked and tried to focus, there was nobody there.

The spring landscape was different this year. Shoots of a crop could be seen poking above the surface of the water. It didn't look as purposeful as a crop, however, more a random spread of weed but like pond grasses, it seemed to belong and thrived in the wet earth. The plants grew tall quickly: Richard hadn't a clue what they were. They reminded him of sticks of celery; tree-sized celery with a fleshy stem and a few branches at the top. These celery trees grew out of the water either side of the old signal box, and the plantation that no farmer could have planted spread along the length of the railway. The branches thickened and overlapped until the flat, open landscape was barely visible. It seemed that the mosses had soaked up a hundred years of growing potential and spurted out a forest in one spring.

The crop became so prolific it put new shoots up on to the track and grew between the sleepers. Botanical experts came from the university but no one was able to identify the plants. Their habit was of bindweed but the structure much more robust. Like celery the stalks were stringy, but on the main trunks, the strings were more like sisal ropes, reinforcing the flesh.

Then the delays started. At first the railways' maintenance engineers could clear the growth overnight to allow the morning trains to pass. Sometimes they weren't able to finish in time and trains were late arriving in the city. The plants' twisting branches formed thick walls along the track side and arches above it. Light mornings but dark journeys for the passengers through this cloister of vegetation.

Some passengers started to make alternative travel arrangements. More engineers were brought in from districts further afield to work round-the-clock shifts. This gave Richard hope as he didn't own a car and had no other means of getting to the office. The work gangs used the old signal box and a couple of nearby cottages as a base. There was always a reserve team there, day and night, ready to take over when the last was exhausted. Despite this effort, all trains were late. Richard was never home on time. Never had a chance to enjoy his wife's company at the same time as her cooking; his meal was now kept warm in the oven. Much worse was the loss of early evening time with his sons. By the time he got home all he saw were shapes, slumbering under Rovers quilts.

Heavier cutting equipment was borrowed from a local coal mine and the first morning after the journey was smoother and punctual. On its return that evening, however, the train stopped by the signal box. The passengers could see the engineers working hard and resigned themselves to finishing the evening newspapers before they set off again. Then a tentacle began to creep over the roof of the carriage. Then another until the whole train was covered by curling, twisting strands. They tied themselves in knots above the carriage like ribbons round a parcel. The engineers could do nothing. They tried to cut the growth near the doors so the passengers could escape but their equipment was impotent. Just before the stalks covered the window Richard thought he saw the round man by the old signal box; Richard blinked and he disappeared. The green knots tied themselves tighter and tighter, squeezing the carriage like a Play-Doh sausage.

In Marshend, Richard's wife covered a dish of braised celery and put it in the oven to keep warm.

Can You Get a Signal on York Minster?

The cathedral bells struck five.

'Wake up, it's time to do a recce on that new building before the sun gets up.' Dunstan nudged Drogo.

'What about Adam? Is he coming too?'

'Let him sleep, we've not much time or the bishop may see us flying about when he leads out the matins procession. Remember last week when he looked up and spotted Old Adam struggling back to his perch. "If I weren't a believer, I'd swear those gargoyles are up to something," he said, making sure we could hear. No point in arousing further suspicions.'

'But we're only taking our night-time exercise like we've always done.'

'Yes, but people aren't supposed to know that. The bishop's clever. *He* knows we can fly, breathe fire and talk, but he can't let his congregation believe we can. Such paganism. Not good PR for the cathedral.

And he needs to keep his nose clean because of all the opposition to this new college building. At night, we can be mistaken for giant bats but we have to be stone-faced in the daytime.'

'You're right, Dunstan. Anyway, we get our laughs during the day, listening to the tourists. Let's go look at this new building now the scaffolding's gone.'

With the help of Drogo's fire-breath they had enough light to see the outside of the new college but soon, night was lifting and the eastern sky began to turn pink. 'I wonder if Adam's awake yet,' said Dunstan, hurriedly squeezing on to his perch before being spotted in daylight. 'He spends more and more time asleep now. Can't fly as far as he used to.'

'Well, he has been here longer than any of us. I hope what we have to tell him isn't going to be too much of a shock.'

They returned to their perches on the cathedral's north tower.

In fact, Adam was quite unshockable. Over the centuries he had survived all weathers, seen plague, riots and bishops defrocked. He had grown old as tourism had increased, providing much entertainment. Although he often thought Dunstan and Drogo somewhat rash, he put this down to their relative youth, he being older by a few decades. The age gap had coincided with a crusade starting just after he took up residence, causing all work on the cathedral to stop for a time. He opened his eyes as he heard Drogo hiss,

'Incomers.'

'This is our patch,' spat Dunstan, 'our cathedral and now they've allowed these young upstarts in, just over there.'

'Boys, calm down.' Adam stretched. 'You'll upset the monks in the cloister with your racket. What's up? What upstarts?'

'New gargoyles.'

'You mean they've built another cathedral?' Adam was astonished.

'No it's a new college as we thought,' explained Dunstan. 'But they've put a row of modern gargoyles on a parapet above the main door.'

'Perhaps that's what the vice chancellor meant in

that speech about welcoming the new into our ancient university,' said Adam. 'Well it's not a problem, it might be nice to have a few new neighbours. Bring in some fresh ideas; we are a bit set in our ways.'

'Oh, but they're not like us at all,' spluttered Drogo. 'They're a different colour for a start. Not your nice warm sandstone. They're concrete.'

'And they're not even carved,' added Dunstan, who was a wonderful example of the mason's craft. 'They're cast. CAST! Very inferior. I bet they can't even understand Latin.'

'No, they speak BATS,' chipped in Drogo. 'It says on a plaque over the door.'

'That's not their language; they're the initials of the college. You didn't read the small print, idiot.' Dunstan was scathing. 'It's the school of Business and Technical Studies. BATS. Didn't you see the banner strung across the front of the building saying, "Why not study for an M. Bats?" M. Bats, indeed. I bet that doesn't involve real subjects like Medieval Music, Greek or Archaeology.'

'And they're holding things.'

Adam looked fearful.

'What things? Not weapons? You don't think they're planning a takeover?' In eight hundred years, Adam and his neighbours had survived battles and bombs. He didn't fancy having to face a new enemy with youth on its side.

'No. No, I don't think they're weapons but strange looking instruments. It will need some research.' With that Dunstan yawned and settled down on his perch for a snooze in the morning sun.

That evening, after sundown, all three gargoyles took off towards the new building. Dunstan and Drogo swooped in front of it in a rather intimidating manner. Adam, however, had too many worn edges to look frightening.

'Good evening,' he said. 'We're from the cathedral and thought we'd come over and introduce ourselves as we'll be neighbours now.'

'Sure thing, man,' replied a fresh looking, concrete gargoyle.

Adam gave their names. Before the young man

could reply, Drogo interrupted,

'We've been here eight hundred years you know, not just five minutes. We know a thing or two.' He began to blow flames.

'Wow, that's a neat skill,' said the newcomer. 'Handy on cold, dark nights, eh? By the way, I'm Josh.'

'I think you'll have a lot to learn from us,' Dunstan added.

'Now, now, boys.' Adam could sense his friends getting annoyed without any real reason and he was genuinely curious. 'Now, young man, what's the matter with your ear? Do you have earache? I know a good apothecary who'll have a potion for that strange-shaped growth.'

'No, not earache, that's my mobile phone. Haven't you seen one before? Impossible to do business without it.' Adam remembered seeing tourists walking past the cathedral with these things but didn't really understand what they were.

Now Josh was making introductions.

'This is David, with the briefcase, and this is

Britney.'

'Good grief, it's a woman,' spluttered Dunstan.

'Do you have a problem with that?' Britney stared him out.

'Just a surprise, that's all. We don't have any women on the cathedral.'

'I think you'll find times have changed here,' smiled Britney.

'What's that you're holding?' asked Drogo. 'It doesn't look as if it would be any use in the kitchen.'

'Certainly not,' snapped Britney. 'It's my laptop. I'm here to represent computer science and the wonders of the internet.'

'The internet is wonderful,' added David. 'It helped me find my full name.'

'Which is?' yawned Dunstan.

'David Brent.'

'Who?'

'I looked on the internet for him,' said Britney. 'It said that David Brent was the unforgettable manager in *The Office* and David has ambition, so...'

'Hang on, hang on,' chipped in Drogo. 'Will

someone explain what's this internet and tell me more about mobile phones?'

Into the night, the Cathedral Three had a lesson in some aspects of life in the 21st century.

'So can you really speak to people you can't see with this thing?' Drogo pointed to Josh's phone. 'Hey that'd be good for you, Adam. Haven't you got a cousin halfway up York Minster?'

'I have indeed,' said Adam. 'Haven't spoken to him for centuries. What are the chances, Josh?'

'We can certainly try,' said Josh. 'Should be a pretty good signal up there.'

'Bet that won't last eight hundred years,' grumbled Dunstan. But the others ignored him.

'I've got an identical twin on Salisbury,' said Drogo. 'At least I've heard tourists say so. I've never met him: we were born of travelling masons. Separated before birth.'

'We could check on the internet and see your cousins all over Europe,' said Britney. 'There are some wonderful cathedral sites.'

Drogo had already moved round to look over

Britney's shoulder. 'There's a pretty good view from this one.'

'Drogo!' Adam could see Drogo's eyes were being drawn to more than Britney's laptop. He said to the new neighbours, 'You've been very hospitable, but I think it's time we let you get some rest. May I suggest you visit us on the north tower later in the week? Meanwhile I'll swoop into the bishop's cellar and find us a bottle of mead or something. In return for using your mobile and laptop, we could perhaps tell you some of our adventures: how we survived Henry VIII, Cromwell, that sort of thing? Fill you in on the last few centuries.'

'Sure thing, Adam. Hey, don't let David's businesslike look fool you,' said Josh. 'That briefcase holds a lot of gin cocktails you know. We'll bring some along and make a night of it. See you later.'

Flying home, Adam felt pleased. There hadn't been any scuffles or slanging matches. Drogo had been smitten by Britney so Dunstan had been reduced to sulking on the sidelines. He'd come round. He couldn't go on forever believing that anyone with different origins or younger than five hundred years old had no right to exist. As they settled down, Adam said,

'I think we've a really interesting, bright set of neighbours there.' Dunstan grunted.

'Concrete upstarts with their fancy toys.'

'Well, they were very generous in offering the use of them,' said Drogo. 'I'd like to see more of Britney's laptop any day.'

'You're just a dirty old gargoyle,' said Dunstan. '...and, will someone please tell me... what in heaven's name are gin cocktails?'

The Brick Wall

I hardly slept a wink last night. Kept hearing strange noises. Not scary noises; not intruder noises or police sirens in the neighbourhood. Just odd, dull bumps and rustlings. But it's been a very long week.

Last weekend was our first, full weekend in this house after the move and our first chance for a welcome lie-in. We were both exhausted after the upheaval but I was hoping that once we'd settled, we may be able to revive our flagging relationship. I made tea and brought it to the bedroom. Then I opened the curtains to look out at the trees in the woods behind the house. We both love trees and I'm almost overwhelmed by this view but Bob's been very uncomfortable about it ever since I said I could see the face on the trunk of the oak tree.

'What face? Where?'

'There. Look, in the pattern of boles and knots; see, there's a nose and that scarring underneath just like a mouth and…'

'Don't be daft. There's no face there.'

'Well, it doesn't matter if you can't see it. I shall just think of it as a good spirit of the woods watching over us.'

'You feeling OK?'

'Fine. Why?'

'Even after this move you wanted you're still talking rubbish.'

This wasn't the fresh start I'd hoped for. Despite the much nicer house and the beautiful woods behind, Bob was just as grumpy as before.

I sat up in bed with my tea and looked at the tree. I swear it winked at me.

'Did you see that?' Silly question really as he'd turned over and was nodding off again.

'What?'

'The tree. It winked at me.'

'Which tree?'

'The one with the face.'

'If, when we are in bed, all you can talk about is that blasted tree I'm going to move into the spare room. What time are you leaving for your mother's?'

'When I'm ready. After breakfast. Drink your tea.'

Every so often, I drive north to visit my mum. I spend a few days there and catch up with my sister, Linda, who lives nearby and deals with all the everyday things Mum needs help with. My being there gives her a break and we usually manage to squeeze in a night at the Black Lion.

I put my bag in the car and Bob says, as usual,

'Let me know when you've arrived safely.'

'OK, I'll text you. I expect to stay till Thursday. I'll leave in time to be back before dark.'

One night this week, Linda's husband Jim had a meeting so Linda and I took ourselves to the Black Lion for supper.

'How are things now the move is over?' she asked.

'Not much better. It hasn't given us the boost we'd hoped for, at least not yet. Of course, there's been a lot to do, so instead of spending time together, he's been spending it with his tool kit. It's great that he's willing and can do the DIY jobs but it's like an obsession. He can't seem to stop work and enjoy the place, the surroundings. The trees at the back of the house are really old and amazing. One of them even has a face.'

'A face? You don't mean like those ugly plastic pieces of play equipment in pub gardens?'

'No. It's a real tree with marks on its bark that look like a face. I feel it's watching over us but Bob thinks it's spooky and I'm crazy. I keep trying to get him to talk things through and suggest we walk through the woods together but it's like talking to a brick wall.'

'That's just men for you,' said Linda. 'At least you get the DIY.'

I decided to go home yesterday, Wednesday, and surprise him. I had lunch with Mum, then set off in the afternoon but I hit rush hour on the city bypass, then roadworks, so it was very late when I got back. There was no sign of Bob. The house was in darkness and all the curtains closed. Then I found him, sound asleep in the spare room. I thought of making him a cup of tea but decided he would prefer to sleep. I'd wait until the morning. He never leaves for work early on a Thursday so there would be time for a chat then.

I expected to sleep really well after the journey but then I was aware of these noises, bumping and creaking. Although they didn't frighten me, I didn't want to get up and investigate. I thought Bob may have, but he didn't stir. Eventually, I must have fallen in to a really deep sleep because when I did wake it was 9.30!

My first thought was to make tea. Yes, that's it, make tea and take him some. I put the kettle on and while it was boiling went to the bathroom: quick comb of hair, brush of teeth. Wonder what the weather's like? I pulled open the bedroom curtains – and couldn't see a thing. There was no window. In its place was a brick wall. The bricks were new and the mortar was only just going hard. No window. No light. No view of the trees. But that couldn't have explained the noises in the night; he must have bricked up the window while I was at Mum's. I rushed round to the spare room. It was empty. He'd gone and so were his bags and tools. He'd left before it was light and not opened the curtains. I made tea and took it into the spare room. Had he left a note? No sign. I opened the curtains and nearly dropped my mug. Staring at me was the tree with the face. It had moved. It must have moved itself in the night so it didn't have to face the new brick wall. Then it winked. So now I've moved into the spare room. If Bob comes back he'll know where to find me.

Fish on Friday

Lynne's Friday routine was a day at home with paperwork. This Friday, Lynne could hear water running and was puzzled as to where it was coming from. Surely she hadn't left a tap on? Was that toilet flush playing up again? She walked round the house checking bathroom, kitchen and utility room; all water sources secure.

Then she wondered about the drip-feed system Joe had set up in the vegetable garden. Maybe a connection on the hose had come loose? Lynne went outside to check and found all was well. The vegetables looked healthy, but not thirsty. It was then she realised the water was running on the far side of the fence. She stood on a stool and peered over. She was very cautious in doing this as relations with Geoff, the next door neighbour, had become chilly since the day he had threatened her cat.

'He's a cat, Geoff. I can't keep him on a lead; cats wander where they like.'

'Well I don't want him wandering where he likes near my fish pond. They cost me a lot of money, those fish.'

Despite the fact that Napoleon, the cat, hated water and the pond had a wire mesh over it, Geoff remained very anxious about Napoleon jumping over the fence into his garden.

Lynne and Joe were uncomfortable about this state of affairs as they had previously been on friendly terms with Geoff, inviting him over when they had a barbecue and offering to keep an eye on his greenhouse when he went on holiday. They tried to work out how they could keep the peace as well as the cat.

'I want to be on good terms with all our neighbours,' said Lynne.

'How about we try to keep Napoleon in for a time after Geoff comes home from work?' Joe suggested. 'In the working day he's not here to see Napoleon and now the nights are drawing in there aren't many hours of daylight between his coming home and when he draws the curtains.'

'You mean you haven't seen his security light?'

'You're joking; you mean one of those that can detect movement?'

'Yes, even one as small as Napoleon. He had it fitted yesterday. Told me, very pointedly, "It will detect small intruders".'

'I thought I'd seen everything when he put up the electric fence.'

Geoff was as proud of his flower beds as he was of his fish so had made a small electric fence around them. From their bedroom window, Lynne and Joe had watched him putting it carefully in place. After Geoff had gone indoors they went out to look and couldn't believe their eyes when they read the ankle-high white sign.

Electric Fence. Keep Off.

'Well that should terrify the cat,' laughed Joe. 'Do you think we should tell Geoff Napoleon hasn't learned to read yet?' They collapsed in giggles.

Despite Geoff's attempts at deterrence and Lynne and Joe's best efforts at containing the cat, Napoleon had continued to stroll round Geoff's garden as he did in every other garden in the neighbourhood, except No.7 where there were two spaniels. He ignored the pond but Geoff continued to be anxious about his precious fish and one day had picked up Napoleon and thrown him back over the fence, threatening,

'I'll skin that cat alive if he keeps trespassing in my garden.' There had been frosty silence between the neighbours since then.

This particular Friday, Lynne could see that water was running out of the hose pipe connected to Geoff's outside tap into the fish pond. The pond was overflowing and small fish were being lifted out of the water, through the grill and on to the surrounding pathways and lawn.

'He must have gone out and forgotten about it,' Lynne thought. She ran round to his house and knocked on the door but there was no answer. Geoff's car wasn't in his drive. The gate to the back garden was open so Lynne rushed through and turned the wall tap off. The flow stopped but the fish lying on the ground were floundering. She ran across and tried to pick them up and get them back in the water but they were slippery and thrashing about. Lynne realised this was going to be a long job and there would be casualties but was determined to save as many as she could. Then, Napoleon sauntered over.

'Oh no,' cried Lynne. 'Stay away, Napoleon.'

The cat was certainly interested in the fish but not so much as to willingly get his feet wet. When he tried to approach, Lynne shooed him away at the same time as pushing another fish through the mesh to safety. One fish had not survived. It was lying fishmonger-shop-still on a paving slab, its eyes glazed over. Thinking this would be a distraction for Napoleon, while she saved the others and wouldn't do any harm as the fish was already beyond hope, Lynne changed her tone and indicated the dead fish to Napoleon.

'Here, here, Napoleon. Have this one,' she entreated. The cat seemed completely indifferent. Lynne continued, 'Come on, Napoleon. This one's for you.' She didn't realise she wasn't alone until she saw a shadow looming over her and turning round saw the colour of Geoff's face.

Nude – circa 1920

Every afternoon I have the sun in my eyes as well as the public to contend with. Complete strangers stare and eye me up and down, making the most personal comments. I try to ignore them by looking out over the river to Montparnasse and its new tower where I started out. In those days there were only tenements and studios.

The visitors say many different things about me.

'Her skin looks so tanned.'

Well, Olivia, my alter ego was from the golden South. She must have hated it in that dark, cramped studio; so different from her home. Tiny, high windows and often, only candles for Jules to work by. I liked the candles; their glow wiped out the winter cold.

'She looks goose-pimpled to me.'

There was never any heating there. All spare money after canvas and paints were bought went on wine. At first, Olivia felt the cold terribly. If she complained during work, Jules would put down his brushes and make love to her, so that first winter she complained all the time. Then less often... and just before she left, not at all.

'Her skin has that afterglow from lovemaking.'

Once, he moved, as if to take her to the divan, then stopped and laughed. He lifted me from the easel and turned me to face the wall. I was peeved at having to stare at the walls as he'd painted them a garish, bordello red. This coyness was inexplicably curious. He and his friends denounced every other aspect of prudish, bourgeois behaviour in their conversation, work and lifestyle.

When these friends, painters and their models visited in the evenings, the atmosphere would really warm up, especially after the wine and hash had taken effect. Calm conversation turned to loud and lively debate; always about the future and the latest ideas. Anything to obliterate the memory of the war. Its legacy had been to deny them their young entitlement to a belief in their immortality. Lost friends in great numbers had proven there was no such thing. So they painted with fervour and lived with passion. They no longer had anything to lose.

'The guitar in the corner mirrors her shape.'

Some evenings, one of them brought a guitar. I saw Olivia dance, slaloming among them in the crowded studio, limbo-low in the candlelight, a glass of wine balanced on her brown belly. The guitar often accompanied homeland songs of recently befriended newcomers to the magnet of Paris.

As I matured, I was increasingly admired by them all. I was praised in Italian, Russian, Spanish... until the day I was sold, when they all carried Jules shoulder-high through the streets and spent the night in a stupor on the proceeds.

I have never been turned to the wall since.

Tuesday at Stella's

'Doesn't that woman over there look like Eva Peron?'

I looked to where Tim was staring at the middle-aged woman and her husband, and recognised Stella, whose working hands I had watched from my childhood corner.

The arrangement was, if there was no one at home after school on a Tuesday, I had to join my mum at Stella's. On the way, I would wave to Mr Mitchell in the Co-op butchers, skip round the bottles of paraffin and baskets of firewood on the pavement outside Bates' hardware shop and then slow right down outside the Abbey bakery because the smell of warm ovens was impossible to rush past.

Stella kept a low stool for me in the corner of her front room hairdressers where my mum and other women from the neighbourhood were being trimmed, permed or shampooed and set. Stella's smelled of hair lotions, eau de cologne and damp towels. Sometimes, from my stool, I could also smell old Mrs Canning's feet. Despite being largely ignored by the customers I enjoyed being there, an unofficial member of a club. I always took a book, and with my eyes fixed upon it, was able to eavesdrop on the conversations which continued as if I were not there.

I learned a lot on that stool. Whilst I was as aware as anyone else of the births, marriages and deaths in the district, there were lots of other things I could only have learned at Stella's. The progress of Mrs Watson's diabetes, which one of the Jackson boys was about to go to or be released from borstal, who was courting who, the fact that one of Fred Pearson's pigeons had never returned from a North West Federation race, various accidents at Clegg's mill and who had come off worst in late night scraps outside the Lord Nelson. Occasionally I became aware of a lull in the chatter and looking up would find one or two women mouthing to each other in cotton mill mee-maw. Something too scandalous to risk being voiced in front of me. I soon worked out how to lip-read.

I loved books and spent my childhood working my way through the shelves of the local library. I had one phase of being besotted with stories from Greek mythology, then another of reading *Lamb's Tales from Shakespeare*. My parents encouraged this, it being understood that a scholarship to the grammar school was their first ambition for me. It was a hope I shared; the means of avoiding a lifetime at Clegg's. This was never discussed among the ladies at Stella's, however. No sense in all that education for a girl. After all, they had all had to do their stint in the spinning mill before escaping to the labour ward.

'What on earth are you reading that for?' Mrs Bradshaw asked seeing my Greek mythology.

'Because I enjoy it.'

One day Stella handed me a copy of *Bunty* which her niece had left. I took it to my corner. It was full of stories about girls at boarding school with names like Arabella and Jonquil who played croquet on Sundays. This was another different world; not like anything I knew at all. They even used a different language; 'japes' for what was simply fun and 'tuck' or 'tiffin' for snacks. It seemed just as foreign as the Greek myths but not as exciting. Mrs Bradshaw peered from under her rollers.

'I see she's reading something normal for a change. When she's finished that, Stella, give her a *Woman's Own*. I bet Hercules can't tell you how to make a shepherd's pie.'

Stella smiled at the exchanges between her customers but rarely joined in the gossip. Hardly saying a word but listening to everyone, she concentrated on her snipping scissors and coiling hair round stout rollers.

I thought perhaps Stella was shy because she didn't know her customers very well. She and her husband hadn't lived here long, whereas Mrs Canning and Mrs Bradshaw knew everybody's affairs as they had never lived anywhere else. There was a discreet blind at the front window which let in the light but ensured that passers-by could not identify the heads under the dryers. I remembered when old Mr Dobson had lived in the house and used to stare at everyone from behind grimy nets. My friends and I would run past, giggling. When I realised he wasn't there any more I asked my mum.

'He's been taken away to a care home; he's reached the point where he can't look after himself any more. It's very sad. He was shouting that he had to stay and wait for Dennis to come back from the army.' I later heard in the Post Office that Dennis hadn't come home since Dunkirk. The house was painted and Stella and Bill moved in.

Stella was a real presence in my life but Bill was largely invisible. He worked as a travelling salesman, often away from home during the week or getting back late.

'Lovely weather for you at the weekend, Stella.'

'Yes; we walked all the way to the South Shore on Sunday.'

From my stool I learned all about Stella and Bill's bungalow at Lytham St Anne's where they spent every weekend and eventually planned to retire. I had never known anyone with two houses before and asked my mum if they were very rich.

'Well they're not millionaires but they've got more money than most because they haven't had any children. Anyway, they only rent that house from Mr Dobson's relatives while Bill's job is based in this area.'

Stella's hair was naturally blonde and she wore it swept back from her face in a French pleat. It was a style that didn't need any perming or roller setting.

'Is your hair very long, Stella?' I asked.

'Halfway down my back but it's easier to wear it up for work.'

Then I saw her double. In our living room. My dad was at the table with his stamp collection.

'Who's that? She looks like Stella.'

'That's Eva Peron.'

'She must be a queen to be on a stamp.'

'No, she was the wife of the ruler of Argentina. She's dead now.'

'Is he the king?'

'No. He's a dictator.'

From these conversations with my dad I learned a great deal about the world beyond our own surroundings; beyond Stella's. The stamps I loved most were triangular with beautiful pictures of birds and butterflies. They came from Hungary which only a few years before had been invaded by the Soviet Union.

'More dictators,' my dad said. He had a thing about dictators, but then he'd fought in the war 'to try to stop one'. I thought Hungary was a funny name for a country as it sounded as if the people didn't have enough to eat. Chile sounded cold and Turkey like a Christmas dinner. The likeness between Stella and Eva Peron was striking. As I was learning how Eva Peron had become an icon for the people of Argentina, I could see how Stella gave my mum, other housewives and local mill girls an afternoon's escape from the monotony of their daily lives. They left her house feeling like Elizabeth Taylor or Ruby Murray. My mum would sing whilst getting the tea ready on a Tuesday and felt satisfied that her glamorous look had been achieved with great enjoyment and only a little borrowing from the Family Allowance.

The following Tuesday the conversation was dominated by one event.

'Didn't she look beautiful?'

'He's a good looking fellow.'

'I wonder what that dress cost?'

The headlines on the women's magazines read *Fairy Tale Princess*. Princess Margaret had married Anthony Armstrong-Jones a few days earlier. This was the first royal wedding since the introduction of TV for most people, so everyone at Stella's had seen the broadcast. My dad got some special stamps called 'First Day Covers'.

'Whatever it cost, it will be us that pays for it in the end,' grumbled Joan from the Post Office.

'Well, I don't mind helping to pay for the Royal Family,' replied Mrs Bradshaw. 'It's better than having a dictator.' There was a general murmur of agreement and more discussion of the bridesmaids, what the Queen Mother was wearing and how wonderfully behaved the horses were. There was only a brief mention of Ellie Harris from Viaduct Street who, the previous Saturday, had married Joe Naylor at her father's insistence. They were both aged seventeen.

'And they'll be parents before they're even old enough to wet the baby's head in the Lord Nelson,' tut-tutted Mrs Bradshaw before returning to the subject of the Queen Mother's hat. That evening I asked my dad why we would be paying for Princess Margaret's wedding and had my first lesson about Income Tax.

By the time I was at the grammar school I had really outgrown Stella's stool. I would try to look as if I were concentrating on my homework even though it was difficult to balance all the books and write well.

One Tuesday Stella said,

'There's an empty chair today if you want it.' Mrs Canning wasn't there. On the way home I asked Mum about her.

'She's gone into hospital to have some tests.' I didn't really understand what hospital tests meant. The only tests I knew were for spelling or mental arithmetic. Although a nuisance, they were soon over with so I fully expected Mrs Canning to be back the next week but she wasn't so I had the chair again. Mrs Canning was now recovering from an operation and we all signed a get well card. After a few weeks she returned but didn't look as if she had got well. Her hair was even greyer than before but Stella seemed to take extra trouble over it. She suggested changes; perhaps a bit shorter at the sides, or slightly more curl on top? Mrs Canning agreed but half-heartedly, as if a new look wouldn't really make any difference.

As I got older my mum let me have a key to let myself in after school on a Tuesday but I still went to Stella's as I was becoming much more interested in the local gossip and scandals. There seemed to be more of them since Joan from the Post Office had become a regular Tuesday customer. She would escape after the 'Family Allowance stampede' leaving her mother in charge for the afternoon. She spent the rest of the week behind the counter absorbing gossip from the queue in front of it. She would come to Stella's full of new anecdotes which she passed on with relish. She told us how two of the

Jackson boys had been taught to play the guitar by a prison warder and since their release had formed a band with some of their mates.

'I can't understand why the vicar lets them practise in the church hall,' grumbled Mrs Bradshaw.

'It's the quickest way of getting rid of the mice.'

'They call themselves *The Fortune Tellers*.'

'Should be *The Tea Leaves*.'

Stella gave me a chair from her dining room to sit on as Joan now occupied Mrs Canning's chair. Our card hadn't worked. Joan told us about one of Mrs Canning's granddaughters, Annie, who had recently started a new job. I knew Annie Barton quite well as she was only a few years older than me.

'She's in your Bill's sales office,' Joan said to Stella.

'Oh, yes, I know. Bill gives her a lift home sometimes.'

Although it was a struggle to manage to write and hold my books on the dining chair, I enjoyed going to Stella's. The gossip and laughs made it a very different world from school where everything was regulated and conformity to a strict moral code was expected. At school we all knew of girls who had had to leave suddenly and disappeared to 'the country' but the reasons why were not openly discussed. I just thought the reason was because their dads, unlike Ellie Harris', didn't want them to get married. Sometimes they came back to school the next year as if nothing had happened, except we all knew what had.

'Oh dear! I've left the Family Allowance book at Stella's,' said my mum one Tuesday tea-time. 'Pop round and pick it up, please, love.'

Stella answered my knock wearing a silky, crimson dress and with her hair loose. Her lips and fingernails matched the dress. As she asked me to step into the hall and went to find the book, I heard a car pull up outside and its door slam. I turned to see a tall man with a moustache and carrying a briefcase stride up the path and right into the hall. He looked straight at me and smiled.

'Well, hello; do you live round here?'

'Yes, Stella does my mum's hair,' was all I could

say. I didn't really know how to make conversation with a man who wasn't my dad. Stella returned and handed me the book.

'Hello, darling,' Bill crooned, and leaned over me to kiss Stella as if I weren't there. In the narrow hall this meant I had to breathe in and squeeze against the wall to inch my way towards the door. I accidentally brushed against him and this seemed to remind him I was there. He looked me straight in the eye and smiled.

'Oh, I am *so* sorry, where are my manners?' and he stepped outside and held the front gate open for me with a gallant flourish.

'Busy day, Stella, sweetheart?' was what I heard as I walked away but what I felt were his eyes all over my gym slip.

There was a quiet afternoon at Stella's. All the regulars were there but I got the impression that most of the talking had been done before I arrived. I tried to lip-read the silent conversations and could just make out something about Annie Barton. I quizzed my mum on the way home.

'Oh... er... well... Annie's gone away to the country for a while.'

I feigned innocence.

'A few girls from school have gone to the country. Perhaps I could try it sometime?'

'Perhaps you should try concentrating on your Latin; you'll need that for university.'

I concentrated on Tuesday lip-reading.

Annie Barton didn't stay in the country. She came back and was seen and heard, hammering on Stella's door after dark.

'Mum,' I said, 'I didn't know Stella does hair in the evenings.'

'No. She doesn't.'

On the Tuesday of the next half-term holiday, Mum said she wasn't going to Stella's that afternoon. Nobody was. It was Mrs Canning's funeral and we were all to stand outside until the cortège passed and then follow it to the chapel. Mr Canning had been a coal merchant and his sons still ran the business. They had smartened up the cart and groomed and dressed their two horses to pull the coffin. On a work day the nags looked really scruffy and sad but that day they had been brushed till their black coats were silky, like washed coal. They had ribbons and feathers plaited into their manes and their tack and brasses shone. They could have done justice to the parade at Princess Margaret's wedding.

The family and Pastor Manning walked behind the cart and as they passed each house, friends and neighbours joined the procession until it stretched right back up the street. Suddenly, the horses pulled up. There was a big removal van half blocking the road and the horses, working in tandem, couldn't see their way round it. The van was right outside Stella's. Stella and Bill were both helping men to load boxes into the van. They saw the procession and stood side by side in shock as if glued to the pavement. They stared at the horses in their finery, the pastor, the coffin and all Mrs Canning's relatives behind it. They saw her neighbours and the women she'd worked alongside all those years at Clegg's and the Tuesday ladies and Mr Mitchell from the Co-op and Mr Bates who'd supplied her with paraffin for forty-five years.

Then Mrs Canning's son-in-law who was Annie Barton's dad, rushed up to Bill. I thought it was to ask him to move the van over but Mr Barton raised his voice and his fist and shouted something and the pastor and Mrs Canning's sons had to pull him away and push him back into the procession. Stella fled into the house. Bill asked the driver to move the van, followed Stella and slammed the door shut. A mumble started and worked its way back up the crowd. The horses moved on.

'Well, well, Edith,' said Mrs Bradshaw. 'I bet you didn't realise your funeral would give us the most excitement we've had since the Coronation.'

'Don't Cry for Me, Argentina' was all over the air waves. I was newly married to Tim and working for a business consultancy. I was the only girl from my street to go to university. I never learned to make a shepherd's pie. I had moved away.

Tim and I and a group of friends were in Blackpool. We were having a day in the sun before going to the theatre to see *Evita.* It was May, too early for crowds so the ten of us must have looked quite a mob as we sauntered along the front, laughing and overspilling the pavement. That was when Tim spotted Eva Peron's double.

'Look, she's just like her.'

'Yes. I think it's Stella.'

'Who's Stella?'

'Someone who used to live near us when I was growing up.'

'Ha! So she escaped too?'

As we clustered round an ice cream van I watched Stella and Bill as they sat on a promenade bench. I was just one of a noisy group and I doubt she would have recognised me. Stella still looked dignified and elegant, exactly as I imagined Eva Peron would have looked in her fifties. I suppose disappearing from our neighbourhood was an escape for both her and Bill. I wondered if Mr Dobson's was the only house they had had to leave in a hurry? How many Annie Bartons had there been?

'Yes, she left.'

'Good for her. She looks far too smart to be stuck

in your old neck of the woods with its tribes and traditions.'

'Well, we all looked after each other,' I said, defensively.

'Only if you toed the line.'

Tim's comment reinforced what I already knew. I had broken the rules by leaving for an education and career which probably meant I would never go back. Mrs Bradshaw had challenged my mum in front of everybody in the Post Office.

'What was the good of all that schooling if she can only get home to see you for the odd weekend?' Mrs Bradshaw's sons had never managed to move away but one by one, her daughters-in-law had.

Whatever had happened to Stella since her forced flight, she looked content. Every so often, Bill would look up and his eyes would settle for a few moments on a passing girl but they always returned to Stella. Despite being older now, they were holding hands, completely bound up in their self-contained world; caught like a hook and eye.

Late for Life

He was born late, six days overdue and about as late in the year as one could be – two minutes to midnight on New Year's Eve.

He remembered his mother retelling the story throughout his childhood. How she had dressed in her finery as she believed, after all, she would be able to attend the Salisburys' New Year party. It was on the way there that they had to make a detour to the maternity hospital.

He was an only child, and growing up in the creaky, old house surrounded by fields, spent most of his early years with adults. At school he didn't easily make friendships with other children. Although a reasonable scholar, he never excelled at anything. On the rugby field, he was always a substitute, coming on late in the game to keep the numbers up.

Believing himself to be a late developer, he drifted but took a degree in his late twenties. At university he met a young woman. At first, his reticence allowed him to only look at her with longing. When he finally asked her out for a drink and she accepted, he realised he was passionately in love with her. After weeks of dithering and wondering how he could take the relationship to another level, she announced she was going to Australia.

'I've been offered a job in Sydney. I've a cousin I can stay with.'

He was so shocked he was unable to respond. At the last minute he dashed to the airport, hoping to find the words to persuade her to stay but roadworks and rush hour meant that when he arrived, too late, she had already boarded.

Time passed. He got an interesting job and made friends but could not forget the young woman he felt destined never to see again.

Then his mother became ill and clearly wasn't going to recover. He spent long afternoons with her while she talked about the past, his late father and the changes in the world around them in the old house that hadn't changed. He asked her about his birth saying he had always worried that the lateness and timing of his arrival had inconvenienced her. His mother laughed out loud.

'Not at all. If you had arrived on time you would have messed up Christmas. As it was, I had a lovely, lazy day with your father. I also avoided being pestered by local newspaper photographers wanting Christmas baby shots. Those New Year parties at the Salisburys' were always such a bore; I was glad of the chance to escape one. You came just at the right time. Now, pour me another gin please, dear.'

This revelation astonished him. All his life he had always felt behind, missing out because he felt his destiny was to be slow to catch up and catch on.

Once he had settled his mother's estate, he booked a flight to Australia, found a hotel via Late Rooms (old habits die hard) and sought out his friend from university. To his surprise, she was delighted to see him. He tried to find the words to explain how he regretted not persuading her to stay nor following her sooner, but faced with her mature, striking beauty, he was mumbling and incoherent. She let him struggle for a few minutes then put her fingers over his lips, smiled and said,

'It's never too late.'

Guava with Garlic

The painting was to give me the idea. I was at one of those local library summer art exhibitions. You know, where some of the paintings are so awful that you're immediately relieved of any lingering regrets at never having learnt to paint. The watercolour was called *Still Life*, but it looked more dead than still. The water used must have come from the most polluted reaches of the Mersey, resulting in a range of mud shades. But the subject matter suggested something else. The bowl contained peaches, oranges and plums. There were also the berries of late summer, implying a rich maturity with sumptuous juiciness. On one of the ripe plums was a wasp, having just spotted a handy lunch. But the colour was missing. The berries were grey and the peaches dull ochre. There was a promise of rich flavour but an utter lack of visual appeal. I tried to imagine what had been in the mind of the artist to produce such a contradiction. Was it deliberate or was he simply incompetent? This painting reflected the exact opposite of my own philosophy about food.

I am a keen cook. I love to feed and delight. I believe that food should look superb as well as taste delicious. The eye-catching arrangement of ingredients on the plate, laid on a handsome table is vital, even at the simplest supper party. Colour, shape and texture enhance one's enjoyment of flavour, for nothing can taste good if it has the appearance of the average school dinner. My dishes remind you of Matisse rather than the National Curriculum. Before the first morsel is on the fork my guests are besotted and I can smell success long before the tomato and watercress salad has given way to the saffron paella.

It is a successful recipe, for my friends and colleagues gleefully accept all invitations. I live alone but weekends find my table surrounded by small groups of admiring guests eager to sample my latest experiments. They are more than happy to be gastronomic guinea pigs. At first, I served a combination of foods which were not especially unusual. Grapefruit and celery salad as an accompaniment to fish, or the always fresh-tasting melon with Italian ham and cheese. Then as my experiments were greeted with even warmer approval, I tried more outlandish combinations. Here I began to use colour contrasts as the sole criteria even when culinary conventions were defied. So my visitors sampled kiwi fruit with tomato, lettuce with mango, and one evening, frog's legs with glazed figs in fennel. I enjoyed teasing the minds of my guests as well as their taste buds; so, a guessing game...

'What have we here?'

'Turtle in peach syrup,' I quip, when really it's guava with garlic.

After these gatherings had been going on for some time, each with a different combination of a few people from the same wider group. I realised that no one had ever complained about any dish. Not at all. Had I consistently produced culinary miracles?

Unlikely, as many of the recipes were first time experiments. Or are my guests over-polite? It's neither. My guests seemed to have universally adopted an 'Emperor's New Clothes' attitude to my food. No one wants to be the first to offer any adverse criticism. Their flattery is sometimes extreme but I'm not taken in by it. I believe they now use my house as a sort of unofficial club. It's safe, cosy and they get an excellent menu. I do feel frustrated, though, by the trap I have created for myself by being too free with my flavours before really knowing if I would enjoy the small talk of these people, and their talk is very small. Whichever combination of individuals I invite, I still draw a set whose conversations revolve around such topics as time-share prices on the Costa del Sol, the spiralling costs of skiing holidays, and (a real stunner one spring) a heated discussion on the merits of various makes of lawnmower! It irritates me now to think that by indulging my love of cooking, I have surrounded myself with a set of self-interested bores, thus restricting my own conversational opportunities. I have created my own spider's web with no easy possibility of escape. I can't simply stop inviting them. The evenings are too much of a regular feature of all our lives. Too regular. Too predictable. I decided to try a series of changes, hoping that as time went on, they would, one by one drop out of the set.

For a time, I served dishes whose ingredients rhymed. Beef with cloverleaf following fish with radish. I devised such sweets as pear éclair and a salad, aubergine with praline. One evening it was a simple roast with toast. This didn't work. My guests were as enthusiastic as ever.

Then I created even less appetizing dishes by using ingredients whose names began with the same letter. I made mushroom meringue, beetroot in Bacardi, lamb chops stewed in liquorice. To no avail. All were especially impressed by pigeon porridge! I had to think again. Then I remembered the painting and I thought of changing tactics and, perhaps, my table mates. I could use a different set of principles altogether: deliberately make the dishes look unappealing. At the same time, continue to combine unexpected combinations so as to let my guests down gently.

I decided to get the whole group together one weekend and do my worst. But, not everyone would fit in my flat. I hired a room in a hotel in the next town: a new 'executive' glossy building, all rectangles and fake glass gables. I booked the room by phone and paid cash in advance; a totally impersonal transaction… ideal. I worked hard on the menu (it all had to fit in my car) and deliberated at length over the drinks. Everything had to be perfect.

And it was. The peach with pepper pâté was followed by oarfish with olives. By now one or two of my guests were yawning. To freshen the palate, I served Indian tea sorbet. During the main course of steak with sauerkraut, some were definitely drowsy, but all seemed determined to finish. One or two actually fell asleep over the orange omelette and by the time we'd had the Neufchatel cheese with nuts all were silent. Some had spread out on the floor, others slept where they sat. They looked so calm when struck dumb. It would have been a pity to disturb them, so I slipped out quietly.

Whilst driving home, a little self-doubt crept in. Had I overdone things? Perhaps I should have left it at morphine in the Muscadet? But I did need to be sure, which is why I added hemlock to the Medoc. Hardly any one was awake for the coffee with chloroform and I took the liqueur laced with laudanum home untouched.

Are We Nearly There Yet?

'Are we nearly there yet?'

Meg had only just reached the bypass.

'It's a long way yet, love. I told you this journey will take all day. You've lots of books and toys there to help pass the time. Look out of the window and see how many red cars you can spot.'

The five-year-old gave a resigned, 'OK.'

When she had telephoned her mother and asked if they could come, the response had been,

'Of course. I've told you, you can come and stay anytime. Anytime at all. Your dad will love to have Sean around. He'll take him fishing and let him help around the place. Sean will love all the animals.'

She knew there would be a welcome but needed her mother to say it. Then she'd had to plan the journey; she'd never driven that far on her own before. She reckoned the school holidays would be the best time. Although hot at midday, they could stop and find shelter from the sun. The longer days meant she could still travel into the evening in reasonable light. She aimed to cover the whole distance in a day.

'Why isn't Daddy coming with us?'

'He has to work.'

'All the time?'

'Well, if he gets free days and wants to come and join us he can.'

'Is there a pub near the farm? He won't come if there's no pub.' Meg was at once horrified yet unsurprised by this revelation of her son's insight.

'It's miles from a pub. If he comes, he'll have to drink water or milk like the rest of us. The milk there is fresh from the cows and really creamy. You'll love it.'

'I'm hungry.'

'Me too. There's a town ahead. We'll find a cafe and get some lunch.'

She needed a rest from the driving and a wash and brush up. They were making good time. She noticed an avenue of shops with parking behind. Perfect. The car wouldn't be visible from the road.

There was a cafe. She calculated they could afford to stop for an hour. Sean had always had a good appetite and she watched him as he tucked into sausages and chips. She picked at her omelette.

'It's a long road,' Sean said. 'But I've hardly seen any red cars.'

'When we get back in the car I'll give you the new sticker book I got you.'

'Not dinosaurs again? I can't read their names.'

'No. The night sky.' She knew he spent ages looking out of his window every night before settling to sleep.

'Great; I can show Grandpa where all the planets are. Do they have the same sky where Gran and Grandpa live?'

'Yes but they're out in the country so it will be clearer.'

She remembered the foggy appearance of the sky when she'd moved to the city and how difficult it had been to identify the constellations. So much light-and-everything-else-pollution. She missed the clear skies over the farm. During lunch she kept looking out of the window as if half expecting to see someone she may recognise but they were already three hours away from home. Before they moved on she bought lots of bottled water; it was getting hotter and they would be on open road for a good way now.

'Mum, will Phoebe be OK with Mrs Blackett?'

'Of course, love. She's minded her before when we've been away. She's used to cats and Phoebe gets on fine with her three.'

'Why isn't Daddy going to look after Phoebe?'

'Well, he has lots of work at the moment. He may get home very late and forget.' Greg was hardly aware that there was a cat around the house. In fact, Phoebe avoided him. She hoped Sean wouldn't miss the cat too much but there were lots of other animals around the farm and he'd get plenty of attention from her parents and brothers.

The road stretched ahead; at least there wasn't too much traffic. Every so often they would pass picnic stops and see other families resting by the roadside.

She saw a heavily pregnant woman laying out a picnic on a table. Her husband leaned over and kissed her.

It had started when she was pregnant. Horse play that began to turn nasty. Nothing too obvious or it may have been spotted by the midwives. Greg was aware that he was no longer the centre of her world. Once Sean was born, she was more vulnerable. She had given up her job so was stuck at home with no money of her own. It was impossible to visit her family. Such a long way away. Once, her parents had visited to see their first grandchild. Her father had entertained Sean joyously.

'While we're here we can babysit, give you and Greg the chance to get out on your own some evenings,' her mother had offered. All Greg wanted to do was go to the pub. Once there, he left her sitting with a drink and went to talk to his mates, or watched the match on the big screen. Before they left, her mother had taken her to one side.

'You know you can come to us anytime. There's

always room for you and Sean. We can even help with the money to get to us if you need it.' Meg assured them she was fine. She was too proud to accept money from them even though Greg never allowed her any, apart from basic housekeeping.

At that stage, she couldn't bear to leave baby Sean with a childminder and get a job. In any case, Greg had said,

'Don't get any ideas about going back to work. Your place is here now, looking after my son.'

'Are we nearly there yet?'

It was hot.

'Getting there. We'll be at the farm by supper time. You've been very patient. Try to look out for some place selling ice cream.' From the distance signs, she knew they were making good progress and began to relax about stopping.

'Strawberry, please,' the child replied to the rosy-cheeked woman selling ices and drinks.

'I'll take a chocolate and a bottle of lemonade, please.' They sat under the shade of a tree near the kiosk. She told him about the farm and the house and her old room, the one she guessed they would share.

'Time to go. We want to get there for supper, don't we?' The traffic had built up slightly. Some clouds had appeared and it suddenly got cooler.

'I hope we're not going to hit a storm,' she thought.

'Do you think Daddy will be able to fix the cabinet?'

'I think he'll try, or he may get Jim to help him. He knows about glass.' She had already thought about the possibility of this journey when Greg had come home more drunk than usual. She had been standing by the cabinet; she guessed what was coming and as he punched at her, she ducked. His fist went straight through the glass door. Because Sean was in bed and couldn't be left, Mrs Blackett took Greg to the hospital to have his hand stitched and bandaged. It didn't stop him being able to hold a pint. It was then that Mrs Blackett had had a quiet word and offered to help her get away.

'I can spare it, dear; I only have myself and the cats to keep. Just think of it as a loan; till you get a job over there and back on your feet. The cat's no problem to me; one more won't make any difference.'

Meg was grateful. During Sean's baby and toddler years, it had all been quiet, late at night, when Sean was asleep and Greg was often too drunk to keep steady. Now she feared things may get noisier and the consequences more visible. She panicked that if she were to get seriously hurt, Sean would be left alone with Greg. She accepted Mrs Blackett's offer gratefully. She had just about saved petrol money but the loan would really help her resettle.

Sean had tired of his stickers, toys and books and was dozing. Only forty miles to go. As soon as Jim had picked up Greg for work that morning, she packed quickly. Sean was amazed when she told him where they were going but she hadn't dared say anything before as she didn't want Greg to find out.

'I wanted it to be a surprise,' she'd told Sean when she hurried him over breakfast.

How will Daddy manage without the car?'

'Well, Jim will pick him up to get to and from work. If he needs a car other times, he'll probably be able to borrow a works van.' She felt he would borrow or just take a vehicle and try to follow her. It was only now, when answering Sean's questions she realised by the time Greg got home and found her note, he'd probably be too drunk to drive anywhere and the depot would be locked. The next day was what worried her. But by then her family would know that her visit was to be an indefinite one and her father and three brothers would be waiting for him if he were to show. Greg would know that. He was able to bully her but a tough old farmer with three young sons was another matter. For the first time it dawned on her that Greg wouldn't follow her and she was overwhelmed with relief.

They passed the sign for her home village, drove past the church, the school and the local store.

'Are we nearly there yet?'

'Yes, love. We're nearly there.'

A Night at the Opera

Heather regretted the split with Rob after their three years together. It had been a silly argument but they had both been stubborn and he had walked out. She still loved him.

After the door slammed, she thought he'd be back when the pub closed but it was the next day when he called round to collect his essential belongings, saying he would pick up the rest at the weekend. By Saturday, he was more conciliatory.

'Can't we talk things over, Heather?'

'Colin's sofa can't be very comfortable, then?' she thought. 'I'll make him sweat for a bit,' and stood her ground. He left. Apart from missing Rob, Heather worried how she was going to finance the flat on her sole income, when everything about their lifestyle together had depended on two.

They shared a passion for opera and went to live performances whenever they could afford it. In between, they listened to CDs at home. Paying for opera tickets would be impossible now. Heather was determined to show Rob she could be independent and make him appreciate her. She became very angry, however, when she realised that he had taken most of her favourite opera CDs as well as his own. Now she didn't have the consolation of listening to *La Traviata* or *Tosca* in the evenings.

Heather was tall and statuesque with thick auburn hair. Rob had always been proud to be seen with her. She was as resourceful as she was beautiful. In no time she had placed a small ad in a respectable gentleman's magazine.

Opera Escort

Need a respectable female companion to
be seen with at Covent Garden?
Telephone...

Heather's fees were not cheap but her phone never stopped ringing. The men she escorted to the opera were mostly good company, had plenty of money and all they wanted was to be seen in public with an attractive woman. Heather made it quite clear where the limits of her service ended. She simply offered companionship at the opera. She would not accept dinner, or anything else, from a client. A conspicuous presence in the bar and at the performance was what Heather offered. The client paid for the tickets, her fee and a taxi home.

Some clients were businessmen in London for meetings. One such was Trevor.

'My wife never comes to London with me any more,' he offered. 'She has her own business... too busy breeding poodles; no time for Puccini.'

The most generous and least demanding were elderly and refined, often widowers who simply didn't want to go out alone. Then there were the nouveau-riche types who felt they ought to be seen at Covent Garden but had spent so much time making money they had neither acquired knowledge about opera nor developed any personal relationships. Heather got repeat bookings from Eric, a successful builder, desperate to know more. She enjoyed his company as well as educating him on the finer points of *Faust* and *Figaro*.

Heather still missed Rob but was at a loss to know how to approach him without losing face. Her escort service had become busy and had boosted her finances to a very comfortable level. She had started the escort service to supplement her office wages, enabling her to keep the flat and her own front door. Now she was making so much, she wondered about handing in her notice. Escorting wealthy, intelligent men to the opera was much more fun than assisting with sales campaigns.

One evening at *Die Fledermaus* with a broker from Frankfurt, she spotted Rob. It was obvious he had seen her but she turned away and pretended not to have noticed him. He was alone. She was with hunky Heinrich.

The next week, Henry from Yorkshire contacted her. He was a repeat booking as he tried to get to the opera every time he came to the city on business. Heather had asked about his wife on the first meeting.

'Oh, she hates London. Anyway she's tied up with

a fund-raising scheme for the local Women's Institute. Something to do with a calendar.' Henry was a Mozart fan and tonight was *Don Giovanni*. It was the second time Heather had seen it in a week but she didn't mind as Henry was very amusing company. Then she spotted Rob. He was alone again but it was clear he knew she wasn't. While Henry was buying drinks at the bar, Rob came over.

'Hello, Heather,' he said, pretending he'd only just noticed her. 'You're looking very well.' He stared at the expensive outfit she was wearing.

'I am, thank you, Rob. And you? Did you enjoy *Die Fledermaus* last week?' Seeing Henry returning, she was about to introduce them but Rob made his excuses and rushed off.

The next day Heather's phone rang early.

'Hello. Opera Escort Service. Let me check the diary. Yes, this Thursday 6th in free. *Don Giovanni?* Oh, lovely. Now I just need to take some details.' The voice was American. It sounded faintly familiar. Heather went through the routine of the credit card transaction and finally,

'A white carnation, OK. I'll be wearing a blue shawl.'

In the bar before the performance, Heather looked for the white carnation. It came round the corner in Rob's buttonhole.

'What a cheek,' she spluttered. 'What are you doing here?'

'Well, you've met Benny from our New York office? He's over in London this week and disappointed that he hasn't space in his diary to see *Don Giovanni*. He told me about this stunning woman who escorted him to *The Magic Flute* last time he was in London. He described you exactly and the penny dropped. I got him to make the call for me.'

Heather was quietly pleased at the prospect of spending the evening with Rob but angry at the underhand way he'd arranged things.

'Now I've got your credit card details I'm going to add on a couple of noughts to cover the CDs you walked off with.'

'Now, Heather, that was an honest mistake. When

I cleared my stuff out, you seemed so unwilling to talk things through, I was really upset and just threw loads of things into the bag. Later, I kept phoning you to arrange to return them; honestly, I did, but you were never in. Now I know why. I could bring them back at the weekend?'

'I'm not sure,' muttered Heather.

'You know,' said Rob gently, 'we could talk things through and you may not have to do this any more.'

'What do you mean, "…not have to do this any more"? I want to do this. It's the best job ever. I love it. Yes, come round at the weekend to return my CDs but I am not going to stop doing this, even if it does mean *Don Giovanni* three times in ten days. Do you understand? It's great to be able to go to the opera on someone else's expense account. I'm usually in very good company and it pays well. Perhaps you ought to try it?'

'What? Opera escorting?'

'Why not? There are loads of wealthy women in London, whose would-be influential husbands either hate opera or spend all their evenings at meetings or golfing dinners. Then there are the foreign wives of visiting businessmen. Many are very cultured and probably bored by constantly being carted round as trophies. A safe male escort in a public place would be marvellous.'

'It never occurred to me,' said Rob, 'but it's worth a try. I could do it along with the day job to see how it goes.'

'Good idea,' said Heather, 'and the money you'll make means you can occasionally afford to escort me.'

'Just like the old days, then?'

'We'll see,' she replied. 'Come round at the weekend and we'll talk it through. Perhaps we can get tickets for *The Marriage of Figaro*?'

Rob didn't contact her at the weekend, nor the one after. Heather was surprised by how upset she felt about this.

'I just wanted him to sweat a bit,' she thought to herself. 'Make him think I wasn't too keen to have a reconciliation. What will I do if he doesn't come back at all?'

Her next opera outing was with Felix, a financier from Luxembourg. He was middle aged, not much to look at and very dull company. In the bar at the interval, when Felix was at the bar, she spotted Rob with a stunning woman. She was tall and blonde and when they came within earshot, Heather could make out a Scandinavian accent speaking excellent English. Then she disappeared to the ladies' room.

'Hello, Rob.' Heather surprised him. 'Enjoying the performance?'

'Yes, very good, thanks,' he replied coolly.

'I see you've started escorting.'

'Oh, no. That's not really got off the ground yet. My ad is being published for the first time this week.' He named a respectable ladies' magazine. 'Astrid has come over from our Stockholm office. She loves Mozart.' Heather was lost for words but just at that moment Felix returned and escorted her to a quiet corner. She couldn't believe how jealous she felt that Rob was seeing Astrid for personal reasons, not business at all. She remained so upset, that the next day when a potential client phoned, she told him she was unavailable that night. She couldn't face anyone.

Heather bought a copy of the magazine Rob had mentioned and sure enough his ad was there. It was very professional. She spent a few quiet days doing some soul-searching and planning.

Rob had his first opera escort job. He was very nervous as he waited in the foyer.

'Hello, Rob.' Heather appeared. 'You're my escort for the night.'

'Heather?' He stared at her low-cut dress and beautifully arranged hair.

'How's Astrid?'

'Astrid? Oh, she's gone back to Stockholm. She was only here for a training course. You weren't jealous were you?'

'Of course not but you need training. I'm here to advise you about the finer points of escorting. You know, dos and don'ts: help you get going. The first rule is don't stare open-mouthed at the client. Smile and get her a drink. Mine's a G & T.'

Peace and War

The wind raced across from the east. With no trees to dilute its force it stabbed through the holes in the wire mesh of the border fence. Karl had difficulty lighting his cigarette. It was going to be a long cold night. Soon he heard familiar footsteps.

'Do you think it will snow?'

'I hope not, my friend. At least not before I'm back in the barracks. Here, have a cigarette.'

Lars accepted. They both laughed as Karl tried to push the cigarette through the holes in the fence with his great woollen gloves on; then more laughter at Lars' attempts to light it in the gusts.

'I heard there's talk of a peace treaty.'

'That was the rumour in our huts today too. Perhaps we'll get medals for manning this part of the border so well. You on your side, me on mine? No invasions here.' They both laughed again. This was not a part of the border that either army had approached. All the action was far away between archdukes and politicians playing power games over more lucrative territories. Until the war there had been no border in that place. The people on either side shared a common language and folklore and even used the same town for trade until the arbitrary fence had been put up on the moors and foot soldiers from each side had been sent to patrol it. Both Hans and Lars knew their daily patrolling along a stretch of a few kilometres was a farce.

'At least we weren't sent to the front.'

'And it is beautiful here in the summer.'

'We get free cigarettes.'

'It will be good to get home though.'

'What will you do, Karl, if it is all over, this war?'

'Go back to the farm. Perhaps we can continue with the plans we had before the war. My father was keen to expand and we have fields we've never used to the full. "People always need food," he used to say. I have two brothers, so once we're all back together, we shall have the manpower. And you, Lars?'

'Well my family wanted to develop their business

too. My uncle spent some time in America before the war. He worked in the motor industry which had just taken off there. He came back full of enthusiasm about engines. He can build an engine from scraps. He started to teach my father, my cousins and me. He said the use of motor vehicles here would have so much potential for business. Distribution, you know. If this war really is over there will be trade channels opening up we could never have imagined before.'

'But what exactly will you distribute?' asked Karl. 'We always managed with the horse and cart.'

'Yes, we shall need to make arrangements with suppliers but there will be more people to feed within a year or two of the soldiers coming home. You must know this, otherwise why expand your farm? And how are you going to get all the extra produce around to the markets and wholesalers if you only have a horse and cart?'

The two men looked at each other.

'Perhaps we should introduce my father to your uncle?' said Karl.

'Where is your farm?'

A few miles from Aldburg, only about fifty kilometres north of here.'

Lars laughed. My home is in Maristadt, just down the road from there. One day, just after the war started we found the border had moved and this fence had been built. That's why I ended up on this side of the border and in the opposing army. My grandmother says that throughout history, every time some archduke had a spat with another, they shunted the border around and started to fight over it.'

'Yes, but the fighting never extends this far north. The people just get on with life as always even if they do occasionally find half their town is suddenly in another country.'

Both men laughed at this aristocratic madness.

'Let's hope the treaty puts it back as it was. Then we really can both be on the same side.'

Lars opened a new pack of cigarettes and they each went on their patrol walk, thinking about their prospects in a peaceful world.

After the treaty, the old border was restored and the

fence brought down. The need for food and development of the economies of all the affected countries was so great, governments were giving grants and loans to farmers and entrepreneurs to help everyone get back on their feet. Within a few years of the war ending both Karl's and Lars' families had fulfilled their plans and had collaborated successfully. Karl's father's farm expanded and by using Lars' family's new vehicles was able to deliver the produce quickly and to a wider area. Lars, or one of his cousins, was at the farm daily collecting eggs, milk and cheese for transportation to all towns in the region. They also provided the lorries to take stock animals to market. Social contact between the two families developed and one of Karl's sisters, Yolande, had even been taken on by Lars' uncle as an apprentice mechanic. Lars' sister Hannah and Karl's brother Ivan became very fond of each other. Over the following years, both businesses thrived.

Then something went wrong. There was a misunderstanding between Lars' uncle and Karl's father. In years to come, no one could remember what had caused the problem but a rift developed and it affected both families catastrophically. Karl's father stopped using Lars' family's lorries to transport goods. He didn't realise the difficulty in finding another haulage firm. There were still not that many around. The farm lost customers and was left with produce for which there was no accessible market. Lars' uncle had other users of his lorries but not many. He had relied heavily on the farm as it had become the largest in the area and provided far more business than all the other small companies he dealt with. He found his lorries lying idle in the yard. Ivan was forbidden to visit Hannah and Yolande lost her job.

Hannah, however, was not going to tolerate this warring among her elders.

'I spent my teenage years living through the war, cold and hungry. That was because of stupid men in the capital. They gave us no choice. Now there's peace so I'm not going to put up with that again because of stupid men in my own family who feel it's OK to be at war with each other over some silly business matter. Why can't you make your peace?'

The next day, she and Ivan eloped. She left a note saying they would not return until the two families had sorted out their differences. Although both families were shocked at this development, it didn't change anything and the hard times continued in an atmosphere of stubborn refusal to negotiate. The young men and women of both families married and new children were born. Their childhoods were shadowed by the vendetta and a lack of comforts.

When the next war came, the new generation of young men were glad of the opportunity to join up. Barracks, uniform and square meals were better than the hardships they had experienced during the lean years of feud between their elders. However, things at home then improved. Lorries were needed for the war effort and so the haulage business was busy again. Food was needed for the army training bases in the area and the farm, now Karl's, was known to have capacity. The problem was in managing to fulfil all the contracts when the young men were no longer available to work. The border moved again and a new fence was built.

On patrol one night, young Hans shares a joke with his opposite number over the fence. They exchange cigarettes and what news they have about the war, which is not being fought anywhere near their patch. They discover that they both support the same football team and were brought up not far from each other. Hans can't wait to get home as his family's haulage business is doing well as a result of the war and he has always loved fixing engines.

'We always had lorries around in the yard. My uncles taught me how to fix and maintain them. I'm wasted here; the army could have used me on maintenance. Still, it's probably safer than being blown up in a jeep somewhere.'

'I would rather be working on the farm,' says Karl junior. 'It's really busy now as the army wants all the food my family can produce. They collect it in army lorries.'

'They're probably our lorries in army livery,' laughs Hans.

The two young men share another cigarette and begin to talk about what each would like to do once the war is over and the old border has once again been restored.

'Maybe we should introduce my uncles to your father, Karl?' says Hans.

Plan

23rd July

Dear Stephen

I was very surprised to get your phone call as I thought you were still abroad, but I am delighted you are going to come and visit me again. You were in such a rush to get off the phone once I'd reassured you that your tin chest is safely here with me, I didn't get a chance to give you directions. So I thought I'd send you a plan. Well, I say a plan but I can't draw them very well; I can never get the scale right and I always fall off the edge of the page before I've reached the destination so this is really a step-by-step-find-your-granny-guide. This flat is in quite a different district from the old house, where you used to spend so much time with us. The whole area's new so you won't recognise anywhere. I'll take you past the landmarks you will remember as you go out of the town centre.

When you leave Shawcliff station, you'll notice the changes to the approach. It's a wider road with new shops and office blocks. The statue of Mayor Arkwright still stands at the end though. I wish I'd been there with a camera the day you and Tommy Mason climbed up and decorated him with football scarves, when Rovers got through to the second round of the cup. At first I thought you'd done it for a lark; I didn't know half the lads in the school had bet you wouldn't do it. Then Mary Dawson said her Frank had nearly worn himself out doing all the jobs he could get to be able to pay up what he owed you. I don't know if you've met up with Frank at all in recent years? He's a prison officer now.

Turn left into Victoria Street and pass the hospital. The ward I was in after my fall in the spring overlooks Victoria Street. The nurses were lovely in there, got me back on my feet in no time. Your dad may have told you I had a little stroke? That's rubbish. I was at a party and had a couple of gins too many, that's all. I've been fine since I got home, as this sheltered unit's all on the level and it's good to have the warden downstairs. Much better than that draughty old house. To be honest, I would have liked to move years ago, to somewhere smaller and easier to keep, but your grandad wouldn't hear of it. He liked to spread out in his greenhouses, shed and study and he could never have parted with his old furniture

After the hospital, turn right into Market Street. Dixon's antique shop is still there. Your grandad bought that tin chest with a lock, from old Mr Dixon, before you were born. Then, much later on, he gave it to you. I think his idea was that you could keep your little soldiers in it but whenever we asked what you kept in it, you just said,

   'Secrets.'

Look in the window as you go past: there may still be some pieces of furniture you'll remember from the house. Young Mr Dixon was very good when I had to clear it. He took everything I didn't want to bring here. I know you may have been interested in them as you've dealt in antiques from time to time but when I moved, you were out of the country again.

   'An extended trip,' your dad said. You must tell me all about it. He was a bit vague as to exactly where you were.

Carry on and you'll reach the market hall. Go straight past it and turn into that little street behind it, Diamond Street. The coffee shop on the right is what used to be Goldberg's jewellers and pawnbrokers where you had a holiday job. I know you were really keen, as you would call in sometimes on your way home and look at all my ornaments and china and ask about my jewellery. I suppose it was a bit like homework?

Go to the end of Diamond Street and turn left into Worcester Way, follow it right past all the shops and you'll be pleased to see that the sports field is still there. They haven't built on that yet. Do you remember helping out at the clubhouse tuck shop on Saturdays? Then on Sundays you'd run your own from the back garden. When you phoned you seemed surprised to hear about the new clubhouse. It's quite different from the old one; all concrete and wire mesh shutters at the windows. A reflection of the times some may say. You know we had the most terrible storms and gales last autumn? Part of the old clubhouse roof blew off, then, a tree fell over and smashed the rest. One day, while they were demolishing the remains, there was a knock on the door. It was George, my old friend Sadie's son. He was the demolition supervisor.

'We found this,' he said, 'underneath the

floorboards in the old hut's toilets. I've brought it because it's got your late husband's name engraved on it.'

Of course, you can guess what it was. The tin chest. Locked. I gave George some tea and scones and we talked about how Sadie was keeping but all the time I could tell he was dying to know how the chest got under the floorboards and what was in it. It's very heavy. You've got some weighty secrets in there, Stephen.

After the sports ground, turn left and you're in Church Road. You'll recognise St Michael's, as it's where we had your grandad's funeral. I was so pleased you were able to come, especially as you'd just got back from being abroad. It was very thoughtful of you to ask if I had all the right advice about dealing with the will, the house and everything. In fact, I was very lucky in having excellent advice locally. Perhaps your dad has mentioned Geoffrey? Well, he's a retired solicitor and we are very good friends. In fact we were very good friends before your grandad died, so he was pleased to help me with probate, the house sale and all the other tiresome things that had to be gone through. I thought I'd introduced you at the funeral? Perhaps not? I know you had to dash off quickly. I noticed your friend saying it was time to go. What a smart uniform he was wearing.

As it turned out, there was enough in the estate to keep me very comfortable so I've been sensible and made my own will. I'll be quite frank, Stephen, by the time you come to my funeral there won't be much left to will to anybody. Geoffrey and I are leaving on a round the world cruise in the autumn. You'll meet Geoffrey when you visit as he has a flat in this complex. Like me, he's very independent so we've decided to keep our own places. What's the point in getting married at our age? After the cruise, we plan to buy a good car between us so we can travel around this country. There are so many places I haven't seen and Geoffrey knows some lovely hotels. We're still not decided on a Jaguar or a BMW. If it were Geoffrey's choice he'd have a Ferrari. That does sound fun but I don't think it would take all my luggage and you're not allowed to go fast enough on our motorways.

Once you've passed the cemetery, there's a stretch called Medway Road, which used to lead right out of the town past the woods and fields but now it's built up with new housing. When you get to the garden centre, turn right and you'll pass a small row of shops. One is A to Z Travel Agents. They've been brilliant in helping Geoffrey and I plan our cruise. Next door is a hardware shop. Would you call in and get a hacksaw, or something for picking locks? I'm sure you'll know exactly what's needed. Then we can tackle that chest over some Madeira.

You are now on Caistor Avenue and we're right at the end. There's a sign saying 'Willow Tree Court' outside so you can't miss it. Sadly there are no willows; they planted holly hedges instead. There's a lot of security to stop intruders, so you'll have to say who you are at the gate and who it is you've come to visit. When you let me know what day and time you'll be arriving, I shall let Vladimir, the warden, know so he can chain the dogs up. He may even join us for tea. He and Geoffrey really look after me.

I can't wait to see you again, dear.
I hope you understand this plan.

Your loving grandmother.

Taking Off

'Now go straight there,' my mum always said when I set out on this particular journey. 'Make sure you don't miss your dad. I'll have the tea ready in half an hour.'

This instruction never varied, but neither did the walk. To the end of the road, take a short cut across the corner of the field (the cows were never there at that time) then over the lane and along the side of the works field. This belonged to Clegg's Mill Sports and Social Club. It was fenced and mowed. Men played football here on Sundays in winter. My dad played cricket on Saturday afternoons in summer. There were notices on the fence telling of forthcoming attractions. 'Family Sports Day 26th May. Clegg's Cricket XI v Faireys Engineering 2nd June'.

Beyond the field were more streets of terraced houses and here I met other kids on the same mission as me. We walked together in a bunch. Someone would always ask the time.

'Is it half-five yet?'

'No. If it were, we'd hear the hooter.' The aim was to reach the top of the rise from where we could look down on Clegg's Mill before the hooter sounded so we wouldn't miss any of our dads leaving work. When we were early we would look back past the playing field to another big mill. This was where our future ambitions lay – it was the Co-op toffee works. None of us could understand our dads, uncles and aunties working at Clegg's Spinning Mill when there was a toffee mill just over the field. None of us were going to be stuck in Clegg's with such a mouth-watering alternative.

Once the hooter sounded we all put our hands over our ears and fixed our eyes on the mill yard and gate. It was a big mill. When I asked my dad how many people worked at Clegg's, he just said, 'Oh, hundreds.' When they all started to leave at half past five, you wondered where they were all going to go. How would they all fit into the streets – or on the bus? Some rode bikes, groups of women walked together with shopping bags, chatting and laughing.

There were lots of men in overalls. Many of them went straight in the pub.

My dad came over the road and up the rise, to where I waited. He was always smiling and held out his hand. On the way home he asked about school and did I know what was for tea? Had the baby learned any new words today?

'No, but I tried to get her to say Monday, cos that's today.'

After tea, Janet, from next door, came to our garden and we played ball against the back wall. Then Janet's mum and dad came out and into our garden. They had a policeman with them. He was going round all the houses, so they brought him to our house to speak to us.

The policeman asked if we were all at home, that is, were all the children at home. We were but it turned out that Philip Garner from Class 5 wasn't. He hadn't come home after school.

'I saw him at school in the dinner queue,' I said.

'Yes, we know he was at school today but he seems to have disappeared afterwards. Will you let us know if you see him?'

'Don't you know Philip's mother, Ann?' Janet's dad asked her mum.

'Yes, I've known her for years. We were trainees together at Cropper's. Poor Marian.'

'There's something else,' the policeman said to the grown-ups. 'There's a prisoner gone missing from Greyhouses Prison. He's from South Ashby so if he's decided to make his way home, he may come close to here. This guy was jailed for child abduction. We have no idea if there's a connection with Philip's disappearance but we're asking you to keep your children in your sight – or at least don't let them go out alone.'

He turned to Janet and me.

'You two girls. Do you go to school together?' We nodded. 'Then you must walk together there and back every day – understand? And don't talk to anyone you don't recognise.' We nodded again.

The next day, all the talk in the playground was about Philip and the prisoner. Had Philip been kidnapped? At assembly, Mr Temple told us what we already knew and we prayed for Philip's safe return. After school there was no walking to the mill. I wasn't really expecting to be allowed to go. The first part of the way when I walked alone was fairly isolated before I reached the others by the cottages. I later learned that they weren't allowed out either. No one was taking any risks. The escaped prisoner's photo was on the front of the evening paper.

By Wednesday, the playground was full of stories about the escaped convict.

'My Auntie Lena said there was someone snooping round her henhouse. He could have been trying to steal eggs.'

'That's a bit stupid. What good are raw eggs to someone on the run? They could easily break and he can't cook them.'

'Annie Evans' neighbour said she'd put a freshly baked apple tart on the window ledge to cool and when she went back to the kitchen it had gone.'

'Well my grandad says things have been taken from the allotments. Carrots and things. You can eat them raw.'

Mr Temple was somewhat more serious at assembly and impressed upon us the need to go straight home after school – preferably in twos and threes if there wasn't a grown-up coming to collect us.

Later, when Janet and I got home from school, there was a police car in the street and policemen were visiting each house. We ran for news. Philip was safe. He had not been kidnapped. His mum and dad had had an almighty quarrel on the Sunday night. Instead of going home after school on Monday, Philip took off for his grandma's in Stonebridge Cross. It was some miles away and he had no money for the bus fare so he'd walked, sleeping in sheds at night. He had not fed on raw eggs, apple pie or carrots but had taken milk bottles from doorsteps and fruit from garden trees. On arrival at his grandma's, he had been given a cuddle, a sharp ticking off, and before he had finished his first plateful of hotpot, had a visit from the police.

The escaped convict had been caught too, nowhere near our town, or Philip's grandma's, but heading towards the hills. He had been walking in quite an isolated spot but passed two men fixing a drystone wall and they recognised him from the photo in the paper.

After tea, Janet and I sat under our pear tree and discussed how Philip had made the journey to his grandma's.

'He must have gone along the bus route to Stonebridge Cross, as he goes there often with his mum.'

'Yes and he'll know the landmarks along the way, and the places where the road turns.'

'He must have had to sneak down back streets and alleys or people would ask why he wasn't at school.'

On Thursday we said prayers of thanks at school, although Philip didn't come back that day or the next. But he did return the following week and everything carried on much as before.

But there was a change. From then on, women

talking over the fence as they hung out washing would stop and change the subject when the children came into the yard. When we went out to play we were constantly asked who we were going to play with and where. Of course, we all thought this was stupid. It was obvious we played with all the other kids, either in the street or the top field, same as always. Things were different. I was not allowed to make my own journey again – the journey to the mill at teatime to meet my dad. I wasn't the only one. Other kids complained that they were kept at home after school now. There were always excuses.

'Read your school book.'

'Keep an eye on the baby.' Previously tough women suddenly needed help from their boys to get the coal in. An invisible curtain had come down over the neighbourhood. Everyday life carried on as usual but its colour had changed.

Janet and I tried to pin down why this conspiracy of grown-ups had happened. It couldn't have anything to do with Philip, who was safe after all. The convict was back in jail, so there was no danger there. It seemed as if the possibility of the two events being connected had caused a panic among the grown-ups. Every child said their parents were much more careful about what was said in front of them at home now. They realised that cross words could cause children to misunderstand a situation and become upset and anxious. Philip's parents were not particularly quarrelsome; his dad wasn't a drinker. They were just like everybody else.

Within a year, Philip's mother had had another baby and his grandma had left Stonebridge Cross and come to live with them. Things settled down and we gradually regained our freedoms. Time passed and we grew older and closer to achieving our dreams of being paid for spending our days in the Co-op toffee works.

Wisteria

From her chair on the balcony, Lucy could smell the honeysuckle climbing up the pergola from the garden below. A new plant, still on its journey to the top of the house. Not like the wisteria whose gnarled branches in its naked winter reminded her of her grandfather's hands. It was as old as he, planted by his parents to celebrate his birth and the end of the war. Now it covered a whole side of the house and had been trained around the windows and doors. The family had lived in the house for generations and the life of the wisteria paralleled theirs. Lucy's father was born there and her mother had come when they married.

Lucy called her grandfather Papa Tom; the name she started to use when she began to talk. She had asked him,

'Why did they plant a wisteria when you were born?'

'Well, I think it was a wish for hope in the future.

The country had just come through a terrible war and at that point, with my arrival, I think my parents wanted to look ahead. A wisteria takes a long time to mature; maybe up to thirteen years to flower. They may have felt it gave them some permanence after all the upheaval and something to look forward to.'

Papa Tom didn't talk down to her and Lucy appreciated that. He spoke to her as another human being, not as a baby.

'Daddy says an apple tree was planted in the orchard when he was born. Which one?'

'Come on, I'll show you.'

'The orchard is full of apple trees. How do you know which it is?'

'I planted it myself when he was a baby. Here, a Worcester Permain.'

'Why did you choose an apple tree?'

'Well, we'd had another war by then and I was lucky; I lived to tell the tale. When the war finished, I married your grandmother but there were food shortages. We expanded the kitchen garden and orchard, and supplied fruit and vegetables to the local shops. Apples were very popular so when your father was born we thought another apple tree was a good idea.'

The honeysuckle had been planted only last year to mark the arrival of Lucy's baby brother, Simon. Apparently the births of only male children were celebrated by the planting of something.

'I remember Daddy planting the honeysuckle last year.'

'Yes, honeysuckle was your mother's choice because she loves the scent. I have to agree, it is gorgeous in the evening and it does complete the picture at that end of the pergola where the wisteria never did quite stretch.'

'Have you finished your breakfast, Lucy?' her aunt called from below. 'We'll be going soon.'

'I don't want to go, and anyway, it's too much bother for everyone. I can stay with Mrs Prior in the kitchen.'

'She has enough to do today. Everyone will help you. You have to be brave.'

Lucy reckoned on a few more minutes before they came to fetch her. The last time she and Papa Tom went out together they had a wonderful afternoon at a puppet show and then he had taken her for an ice cream at Burridge's. She thought of his hands on the steering wheel of the car; wisteria hands, old and bony but firm and sure of his driving. She loved going out with him and appreciated his spending more time with her since baby Simon's arrival.

'It's time, Lucy.' Her mother came and put a black shawl around her shoulders. Uncle Paul carried her downstairs and Mother and Uncle Thomas folded and carried her wheelchair down to the front of the house. Lots of people, all in smart black had gathered and were talking in groups. Cars lined the avenue. Lucy was placed by the rose bed and told someone would be with her in a few minutes. There was a lot of quiet chatter.

Lucy was aware of two men talking on the other side of the rose bed. She was partly concealed by the roses but was beginning to learn how a wheelchair made her invisible.

'They have got him in custody?'

'Oh yes, charged with death by dangerous driving.'

'And the child?'

'She'll be OK. Broken leg and arm but otherwise fine.'

'That's a blessing. No brain damage?'

'No, and only in hospital a few days. She's got a good family to care for her.'

All conversation stopped as six of Lucy's uncles and big cousins carried her grandfather's coffin from the house to the hearse.

After their ice cream, on the way home in the car, Lucy and Papa Tom remembered something from the puppet show and they couldn't stop laughing. Then, there was the bang and she woke up in hospital.

Lucy said again and again that she didn't want to go to the funeral. She didn't want to be lifted in and out of cars while they folded and unfolded the wheelchair and struggled to push it over the grassy paths in the cemetery. She had overheard conversations between the grown-ups.

'Well maybe it's not the best place for a child?'

'But it may help to give her closure. After all, she was in the car with him when he died.'

'Grown-ups talk such nonsense,' Lucy thought. 'Some closure.' She knew she had weeks of exercises and hospital visits ahead of her before she could walk again and no one really knew if her leg would get back to normal. Worst of all there was no Papa Tom to sit with her and tell her stories. She would pretend he was still here and she'd spend the summer sitting on the balcony telling him stories. She would describe all the stupid things the grown-ups in the house were doing and saying and how her little brother irritated her beyond belief sometimes, but was adorable at others. She hoped Papa Tom would send her inspiration when the schoolwork Miss Davenport was sending home was tricky and her parents had no time to help. She looked around at the funeral gathering, everyone in black, silent with bowed heads, a few handkerchiefs appearing. At least after today's formalities they would leave her in peace to admire the wisteria and talk to Papa Tom.

About the Author

Trixie Roberts was born and lived for most of her life in the industrial North West of England before moving to rural Shropshire in 2010. She started writing in the 1990s, had some early competition success including the Liverpool John Moores/Waterstones, and a story accepted and broadcast on BBC radio. Having thus caught the writing bug, she decided to continue and this book is the result. Her work is very much influenced by life in Northern England and many of her stories are set there.

She has worked as a teacher, in human resources and charities. Since the 1980s she has run *Brainwarp*, writing and supplying original crosswords and puzzles to in-house publications. She has also been involved in the production of community magazines and newspapers when living in Liverpool, Greater Manchester and Shropshire.

Trixie is a member of Oswestry Writing Group and Leaf by Leaf Press. This is her first published story collection.

Published Work by Trixie Roberts

Many of these stories have previously been published in *Oswords,* the magazine of Oswestry Writing Group.

Plan was included in the anthology, *Dark Water Lit,* Towpath Press.

Guava with Garlic was broadcast on *Write Now,* BBC Radio.

A Perfect Alibi

R. J. Turner

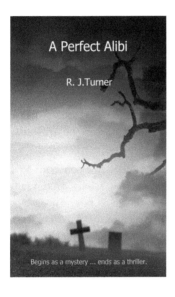

A Perfect Alibi

R. J.Turner

Begins as a mystery ... ends as a thriller.

Richard Downs, an ageing, mid-list crime writer, suffers a severe stroke and dies in hospital, with his daughter at his bedside.

She arranges his funeral, but when his coffin is about to be lowered into the grave a terrible discovery is made.

During the investigation that follows, Jane begins to learn some horrid truths about her father.

'A thoroughly gripping tale from a writer who deserves a wider audience.'
Dave Andrews, author of *The Oswestry Round* and the Himalayan journal *Gobowen to Everest.*

Purchase from www.leafbyleafpress.com

It's Not A Boy!

Vicky Turrell

"It's not a boy!" shouted Posty as he carried the sad news round the scattered houses in the little village of Gum. He was used to bringing bad news in the war and saw no reason to stop.

A girl had been born to a farming family who really wanted a boy. This is the voice of that little girl, now eleven years old, telling her story.

Brought up on a remote farm in Yorkshire in the 1940s and '50s, she shows how her birth was a bombshell to her farming parents.

Living in rural isolation, she saw and interpreted, in her own inexperienced way, all aspects of human life.

To make up for not being a boy she devised a list of things she was good at so that she could succeed and make her parents proud of her. But is her list good enough?

This story was inspired by real events although some scenes and people have been invented for the purpose of the narrative. The language used is of its time.

Purchase from www.leafbyleafpress.com

In Free Fall
Bernard Pearson

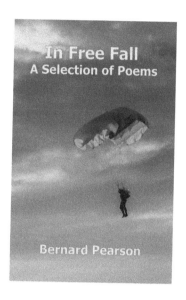

This collection of poems spans forty years, one marriage, two children several breakdowns, and a treasury of friendships. It is I hope accessible, diverting, at times comforting and constructively disconcerting. The poems tell of someone trying to make out whether that is the sky or the ground beneath him.

"In Free Fall gives us Bernard Pearson's distinctive and charming voice at its emotive best. With his command of form, wit and individual sense of music, the poet celebrates people, place and nature, offering us powerful reminiscence, unforgettable endings and lyrical grace."
Jonathon Edwards. Winner Costa Book Award for Poetry 2014

Purchase from www.leafbyleafpress.com

Here and There

W Lodwick Lowdon

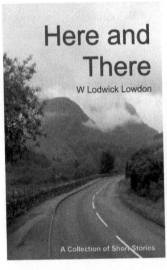

Here and There vividly portrays characters and events set against the back drop of Australia or Great Britain; countries which may be apart geographically but the stories depict the commonality of human foibles.

The stories may differ in tone and culture but in each the focus is on divergent characters occupied by amusing, poignant or difficult situations. The author was inspired by the experience of living half a life in Australia and half in Great Britain.

'Whether in the Outback of Australia or in an English Country Garden W. Lodwick Lowdon casts a wry and perceptive eye over the human condition providing many a surprise along the way.' Bernard Pearson, Poet, author of *In Free Fall*.

Purchase from www.leafbyleafpress.com